A Taste of Smoke

OTHER YEARLING BOOKS YOU WILL ENJOY:

YEARLING BOOKS are designed especially to entertain and enlighten young people. Patricia Reilly Giff, consultant to this series, received her bachelor's degree from Marymount College and a master's degree in history from St. John's University. She holds a Professional Diploma in Reading and a Doctorate of Humane Letters from Hofstra University. She was a teacher and reading consultant for many years, and is the author of numerous books for young readers.

For a complete listing of all Yearling titles, write to
Dell Readers Service,
P.O. Box 1045,
South Holland, IL 60473.

A Taste of Smoke

By MARION DANE BAUER

A Yearling Book

Published by
Bantam Doubleday Dell Books for Young Readers
a division of
Bantam Doubleday Dell Publishing Group, Inc.
1540 Broadway
New York, New York 10036

ISBN: 0-440-41034-7

Reprinted by arrangement with Clarion Books, a Houghton Mifflin
Company imprint
Printed in the United States of America

August 1995

10 9 8 7 6 5 4 3 2

FOR MEGAN,

my Australian daughter,
who led the way out of the night forest.

Chapter One

CAITLIN SQUEEZED HER EYES SHUT, counted to ten, then let them spring open again. The landscape hadn't changed. It was the same checkerboard of farms and trees, farms and trees, flowing away from the car on every side.

"How much farther?" she asked, interrupting whatever it was her sister had been saying.

Pam gave an exaggerated sigh, the one she borrowed from their father for such occasions. But then she said, more patiently than he probably would have, "Not far. We'll be in Hinckley in twenty minutes."

"And at St. Croix State Park in twenty more," Caitlin added, jiggling impatiently in her seat.

Pam smiled then and took her hand off the wheel to pinch Caitlin's knee, just hard enough to make her jump. "If you knew, why did you ask?"

Caitlin smiled back. She shrugged. It had been something to say, hadn't it? A way to break into Pam's endless monologue about the wonders of "university life."

But then Pam went back to talking about one of her professors. He had, she said, "stunning" eyes and an "incredible" mind, though Caitlin failed to see what one had to do with the other.

Caitlin wasn't interested in hearing about Pam's year away at college, not any part of it. Her sister was home now, and that was all that mattered. She was home, and they were going camping, just the two of them.

Their parents had decided, after their last family trip three years ago, that they were *through* with camping. For years Dad had complained about "waking up with the imprint of roots in my back," but the night that a raccoon had broken into their cooler and run off with all the butter and meat, it was Mom who had decided the family trips were over. Caitlin had been heartbroken, until Pam had gotten their parents to agree to let her take Caitlin out. Camping alone together had come to be one of their most cherished traditions.

"I've got an idea!" Caitlin exploded, interrupting Pam's monologue again. "Instead of checking into the park campground, why don't we just go out into the forest and live off the land?"

"What on earth are you talking about, Linnie?"

"I mean" — Caitlin straightened her back; when she did

that she sat almost as tall as her sister — "we don't need tents and food and stuff like that. We can build a little lean-to in the forest and make a bed of leaves. And we can live on berries and fish and . . . and . . ." She was running out of steam. She couldn't think of anything else they could live on.

Caitlin knew even as she spoke that the idea was foolish. Not to mention immature. But then that's the way it was at thirteen. Every time you opened your mouth you said something that people who were older than you decided was either too young or too old for your age.

Pam didn't criticize, though. That was one of the things that hadn't changed. Pam had always treated her like a real human being, not a little kid to be condescended to or corrected every minute. She just shook her head and said, her tone wry, "My sister, the nature woman."

Caitlin liked that word, *woman,* even if it had been said in jest. "At least we can start the fire without any matches, can't we?" she persisted. "Like the early settlers used to do? I'll bet if I find a really hard rock I can strike sparks from it with the blade of the jackknife."

"You can do anything you like with the fire, as long as you have one going by the time we need it for cooking supper," Pam replied, laughing. And then she went back to talking again. About some boy this time.

Pam was pretty — beautiful, really — with a curling cap of chestnut brown hair, perfect skin, and a bell-like laugh that made everyone laugh with her. She'd had a string of boys trailing after her as long as Caitlin could remember.

Trailing boys had never been a problem for Caitlin, and she had only to look into a mirror to know why. Straight, no-color hair, ski-jump nose, and on this particular day, a purple zit erupting between her eyebrows. Her hand sneaked up to touch it again. It felt like the beginnings of a unicorn's horn.

Pam's story about the boy flowed on like the kind of music their mother liked, one tune indistinguishable from another. Caitlin went back to watching the scenery.

She was going to burst if she didn't get a chance to start on her list. It was a mental list, not a written one, and she had been adding to it all year long, waiting for Pam to be home, waiting for this, their first time camping out together.

Dennis Blattner was number one on Caitlin's list. Dennis Blattner wasn't exactly her boyfriend; you could hardly call someone a boyfriend who had never even spoken to you. But he often smiled at Caitlin if she happened to look in his direction. (And she *happened* to look in his direction quite a bit.) Sometimes he even hung out around her locker, trying to act like it was where he belonged or something. When she approached, though, he always melted away into the crowded hallway before she got a chance to speak to him.

Caitlin had tried to talk to her mother about it once, about what she could do to give a boy courage, especially a shy, sweet boy like Dennis. But Mom had just said, "Oh, Caitlin.

Not boys! You're much too young for all that!" As if she were talking about *doing it* or something. And, of course, she'd never even tried talking to her father. He would have been worse.

Pam would understand. About Dennis Blattner and everything else. In fact, Caitlin had planned to start out by mentioning Dennis, just casually, during their drive up to the state park. And she intended to still . . . if she ever got a chance.

"He said we should see the museum in Hinckley before we go on to the park," Pam was saying now.

Who said? Caitlin wondered, but she didn't ask. Instead she repeated, her voice falling like her heart, "A museum." The only thing she wanted to see was their camping site.

"It'll be interesting, Linnie. Really. The whole museum is about the Hinckley fire. They have a film about it and everything."

Caitlin had heard about the Hinckley fire. It had been a long time ago, probably a hundred years. All the land around Hinckley, Minnesota, farmland now, had been pine forest before this one enormous fire had come along and burned up everything in sight.

She sighed. "We won't stay long, though, will we? It's been forever since you and I were camping. If we don't get there soon, I think I'm going to die."

Pam laughed again, a warm, rich peal that filled the car

and even pulled the sun out from behind a cottony cloud. "I'd almost forgotten how you love to exaggerate," she said. But she looked over with a fond expression that took any sting out of the teasing words and reached across to take hold of Caitlin's hand.

"I missed you," Caitlin said softly.

Pam squeezed her hand. "And I missed you, too. A whole bunch."

Caitlin sighed again, with pleasure this time and with the deep satisfaction of being with her sister. It didn't matter, really, taking a bit of time out for the museum if that's what Pam wanted to do.

They had three whole days ahead of them, three days alone. And there wouldn't be a single soul to interfere. Caitlin's list was only the beginning of what they would talk about.

Everything was going to be perfect. Perfect!

*

The movie screen glowed as though the fire were here and now, surging to life in the air-conditioned theater of the museum. Caitlin squirmed in her folding chair and raised a hand to wipe the sweat from her forehead. Startled to discover that her skin was cool, she dropped the hand to her lap again. The flames roared on.

The great Hinckley fire. September 1, 1894. It had been a

wall of flame, several walls of flame converging, actually. Not only the roots, the underbrush, the crowns of the trees, but the very air above the forest ignited. The fire roared, leapt miles into the sky, created its own winds, its own rules. It consumed, obliterated everything in its path, then, strangely, left untouched some shed or plow or tender-fleshed human huddled in a potato patch.

Four hundred eighteen people died. More than that. The dead from an Ojibwa hunting party in the area were never counted. In a matter of a few hours, the booming lumber town of Hinckley, Minnesota, several other small communities, farms and homes scattered across the land, and nearly five hundred square miles of virgin forest were reduced to a charred rubble.

There were heroes, of course. Great disasters make heroes of otherwise ordinary folk.

Thomas Dunn, telegraph operator at Hinckley, stayed at his post, trying to warn others down the line of the coming fire storm. The final message he tapped out was "I have stayed too long."

Engineer William Best carried approximately 350 people from the burning town. He waited until the final possible moment, until the railroad ties were burning beneath his train, before backing away from the inferno . . . and, painfully, from the last poor souls who ran down the tracks, pleading for rescue.

A fifteen-year-old orphan boy had been left at the lumber mill when the men were excused to get their families to safety and to fight the fire. He had been told to blow the whistle if the fire threatened, that the men would return to save the mill. By the time the fire came to the mill, approaching the town from every side, those still alive had found refuge on the train.

The boy, faithful to his station, blew the whistle. The 350 people on the train heard it. But the train was pulling away. There was no one left to save the mill . . . or the boy.

In the darkened room used both for displays and for showing the film, Caitlin squirmed in her chair. Why had Pam wanted to come here, anyway?

The film went on to other topics, but Caitlin couldn't get the boy out of her mind. To be alone in the world like that. To die, waiting for the others to return. She knew it made no sense, but she found herself feeling deeply connected with him, as though she, too, were an orphan left behind by an uncaring world.

When the film ended and the lights came on once more, Caitlin sprang to her feet. "Can we go now?" she demanded. "I'll need plenty of time to get the campfire started before supper."

Pam didn't reply. Instead, she rose more slowly and stood searching the departing audience, though for what — or whom — Caitlin couldn't imagine.

"Are you ready?" Caitlin asked again.

"Not just yet," Pam replied absently. And then she added, moving toward the aisle, "I want to look around a bit more."

Caitlin trailed behind her, exasperated. *Look at what?* she wondered. They had already seen every display in the museum, some of them two or three times, while they'd been waiting for the film to start.

She knew now why the story of the orphan boy had bothered her so. It's the way she'd been feeling with Pam since her sister had arrived home, as though she didn't matter. Almost as though she didn't exist.

Exactly the way the boy hadn't mattered to the people on the train. Did any of them care that they were leaving him behind to die? Or were they concerned only with what was happening to themselves?

An extremely tall young man with a dark beard appeared in the doorway of the room that contained the theater, moving against the crowd. He waved in their direction and, incredibly, Pam returned the salute.

Caitlin stopped in the middle of the aisle, letting the rest of the small crowd flow past her. She watched Pam hurry toward the young man, whoever he might be. What an odd coincidence for Pam to run into someone she knew so far from their home in Minneapolis!

Irritated and wary, feeling abandoned all over again, Caitlin started toward the pair, though she hadn't the slightest desire to meet this stranger. Before she had gone two steps, however, something brought her to an abrupt halt. It was a change in the air. Mist or smoke. Heat waves, maybe. Or else her vision had suddenly gone fuzzy.

Caitlin rubbed her eye sockets with her fists, hard, and looked again. The air directly in front of her rippled, distorting her vision so that Pam, the young man, and the rest of the escaping crowd looked wavery. There was a sound as well. Low at first but growing louder. It was almost like someone crying. Had they started the film again, with the lights still on? She whirled to face the screen.

But the cool screen stared back at her, silent and blank.

The cry grew more desperate, more shrill, until the hair rose on the back of Caitlin's neck. She turned again and started once more down the aisle, only to be brought to an abrupt halt. A wall of fire had sprung up in front of her, cutting her off from Pam, from everyone else in the museum.

Flames filled the aisle, leapt to the ceiling, licked along the floor toward her feet. The fire stood between her and all the remaining world.

But worse, even, than the flame was the voice. "Help me!" someone shrieked from inside that bright burning. "Please! Come help me!"

Caitlin screamed.

Chapter Two

"LINNIE! LINNIE! WHAT'S WRONG?"

Pam's strong arms enclosed her, supported her. Caitlin could feel her sister's embrace and hear the alarm in her voice, but she couldn't stop screaming.

The young man Pam had been talking to was on Caitlin's other side, supporting her as well.

"Caitlin!" Pam said, more sharply this time, and Caitlin gulped hard, managing, finally, to turn off the sound that was issuing from her throat.

In the sudden silence, she stared at the place where the fire had been. There was nothing there. Nothing at all.

Caitlin burst into tears, quieter, at least, than the screaming had been. It was only then that she realized there were other people gathered around, other strangers, staring.

The young man spoke quietly to the watching crowd, and

they began to drift off, craning their necks to keep her in view as they went. Caitlin was grateful to him for sending them away, but she wished he would leave with them. She certainly didn't need him here. Neither she nor Pam needed him.

Instead of leaving, however, he led her back to one of the theater chairs and gently lowered her into it.

"Caitlin, what's wrong?" Pam asked again. She crouched next to the chair to peer into Caitlin's face. The young man folded his great length to do the same.

"It was horrible," Caitlin sobbed. "Just horrible."

"What? What was horrible?" Pam remained gentle, supportive, but there was an impatient edge creeping into her voice.

Caitlin struggled to gather herself enough to explain. "There was a fire . . . right there." She pointed toward the empty aisle. "And someone in it, calling for help."

The young man's face paled behind his dark beard, and he straightened abruptly. Pam drew herself erect, too, tossing him a skeptical look to which he gave no response. Beyond the theater, there was a murmur of voices still. Neither Pam nor the stranger spoke.

Caitlin looked to her sister, pleading mutely, though she couldn't have said what it was she wanted Pam to do for her. Believe her, more than anything else. However unlikely it all seemed, Pam had to believe her.

When Pam spoke, however, her voice was firm and very

certain. "Linnie, you know there was no fire. There couldn't have been one, except for what you saw in the film. And that's over now. See?" With a sweep of her arm, she indicated the screen.

Obediently, Caitlin looked again toward the blank screen — which was irrelevant, of course — and back to Pam again.

"You must have imagined it. Don't you think? I mean, after the film and all." Pam's face, knotted with concern, urged her to agree.

Caitlin shook her head. "No! I didn't imagine it." She took a wavering breath and tried again. "I saw just what I said. There was a fire."

But even as she spoke, she could see, checking the place in the aisle once more, that there wasn't the slightest remnant there of any burning. No ashes on the floor nor even a bit of scorching.

Pam turned to the young man. "I'm sorry, Alex," she said. "I don't know what this is about. Linnie does have these sudden enthusiasms sometimes, but she's usually quite . . ." She hesitated, clearly searching for the word. "Reasonable," she concluded, almost feebly.

Caitlin sat up straighter, swallowing the last of her tears. What was Pam doing, apologizing to this person for her? As if his opinion mattered, as if his opinion were more important, even, than Caitlin's feelings about what was said.

The young man, Alex, looked sympathetic, even pained.

"It's all right, really," he said. "I mean . . . maybe I can explain what happened. What it might have been, anyway."

Pam was clearly relieved, expectant. Even Caitlin held her breath, ready to be rescued from this impossible situation.

Alex hesitated for a long moment, his eyes traveling rapidly, almost nervously, from one face to the other. "It seems to me," he said finally, "that I heard the museum has been experimenting . . . with sound and light . . . you know?" He tugged on his beard as he spoke. "And maybe what you saw," he nodded at Caitlin, "was one of their new special effects. Don't you think that's what it was?" He seemed almost to be pleading with her to agree.

Special effects! That would be better, wouldn't it, than to be told that what she had seen was all her "imagination"? But as much as she wanted to, Caitlin couldn't possibly agree.

"It was real," she explained again, more calmly now. "It was a real fire. Right over there." She pointed once more. "And someone in it . . . calling." She let her arm fall limp and looked from Alex to her sister. Pam could say all she liked about Caitlin's loving to exaggerate, but Caitlin didn't lie. Pam knew that perfectly well.

Pam, however, seemed to be delighted with Alex's explanation. "A special effect!" she cried brightly. "That must be what it was! Don't you think, Linnie?" She beamed at Alex as though he'd just come up with the right answer on a quiz show, the kind where you won all kinds of junk. Then she gave Caitlin's arm a squeeze, as much warning as reassurance. "After all, you don't usually go around seeing things, do you?"

Caitlin jerked her arm free. She had seen what she had seen. If these two didn't believe her, that didn't change a thing.

Clearly, however, Pam had decided that the entire matter was settled, and she began making introductions. "Alex, this is my sister, Caitlin. Linnie, this is a friend of mine from school, Alex Simmons. He lives in Hinckley. Isn't it a nice surprise, running into him here?"

A nice surprise! Caitlin was still jittery, liquid in all her joints, but she had herself together enough to get the picture . . . instantly. It could hardly be more apparent that Alex was no "surprise." He must be the reason they had stopped at the museum, probably the reason Pam had decided on nearby St. Croix State Park as their place to camp.

"Pleased to meet you," Alex said, looking more upset than pleased. He tugged on his beard again, as though reassuring himself that it was still there. "Pam's told me all about you."

All about her? Caitlin rose stiffly. How many of her secrets had Pam given away? And to someone who must be the most casual of friends.

This Alex just wasn't Pam's type. The boys who hung

around Pam were usually athletes, Adonises with golden hair and skin . . . and muscles. Not only was Alex as tall as a telephone pole, he was just about as skinny. Everything about him was long — long arms, long legs. He even had long ears and a long nose. Kind of like Abraham Lincoln.

Come to think of it, Lincoln had been homely, too.

Alex turned back to Pam. "Why don't we go on out to the park? I'm sure your sister will feel better when we get away from this place."

What was this dork talking about, *we?* Caitlin waited for Pam to explain his mistake. Just because she had stopped by the museum to see him didn't mean he was invited to come with them the rest of the way. Neither Caitlin nor Pam had ever let anyone else interfere with their camping trips! Ever!

But Pam was standing there nodding, like one of those dolls with the bobbing heads some people put in the back windows of cars. "Great idea," she said. And motioning for Caitlin to follow, she started up the aisle beside Alex. "We'll be at the park in thirty minutes," she tossed back over her shoulder. "Didn't you want to see if you can start a fire without a match?" Then she rolled her eyes at Alex as if to say, *Isn't my little sister cute?*

For the second time, Caitlin stood in the middle of the empty aisle, watching her sister walk away from her. Where did Pam get off, treating her like that? And what did she mean, letting this guy come along to the park? Or telling him about her idea of starting a fire without a match, for that matter? It sounded so dumb, said right out to a stranger that way.

"You can do the fire," she called after her sister. "It makes no difference to me."

But Pam gave no sign of having heard. She was now pouring out her stream of talk at Alex, who walked beside her with his head carefully inclined in her direction.

Muttering to herself, Caitlin followed. She didn't seem to have much choice.

When Pam and Alex pushed through the outer door to the parking lot, Caitlin caught the door, then turned back to look over the museum one last time.

The building that housed the museum had once been a railway depot, rebuilt after the fire. It was quiet, clean, everything in its place. It was also traditional, even staid, like the neatly laid out town of Hinckley itself. There wasn't the slightest hint of hidden lights or cameras or any of the electronic paraphernalia that would be needed to create something as spectacular as what she had witnessed.

How could she possibly believe the fire that had appeared in front of her had been that kind of trick?

And how could she believe anything else? Flames didn't suddenly spring up, then go out again without leaving a trace. And if there had really been a fire, if someone had actually been burning right there in the middle of the aisle, it wasn't likely that she would have been the only one to see, the only one to hear the cries. None of this made sense. She knew it didn't. Yet . . .

"Linnie!" Pam was standing next to the family station wagon, sun glinting in her hair. Alex stood beside her, waiting, too.

Caitlin shook herself, hard, and stepped out into the harsh light of the summer day.

*

Caitlin sat cross-legged on the ground, well back from the campfire Alex had built. Ten minutes after they had all arrived, he'd had it going. (Though, of course, he'd had to use a match.)

The uncomfortable questions that had begun in the museum had multiplied. Why was it, if the fire in the museum had been real, that the one Alex had built seemed to throw out so much more heat? She couldn't have been more than two feet from the flames when they had appeared in front of her, and yet, she realized now, she hadn't noticed the slightest change of temperature in the air-conditioned room.

But most telling of all, somehow, was the fact that the campfire crackled and snapped, even roared in a subdued way. Except for the voice, the fire in the museum, she realized now, had been completely silent.

Alex must have been right. It had all been special effects.

There was no other reasonable explanation, and she was, as Pam had been quick to explain, a *reasonable* girl.

Supper was finished, and Alex and Pam had settled by the fire, still totally involved in one another as they'd been all afternoon. Caitlin slapped a mosquito feasting on her arm and examined, with satisfaction, the bloody smear it left. Here she had been feeling sorry for herself earlier because Pam had been talking . . . and to *her!* Now it looked as though her sister was going to be talking to Alex the whole time they were here. She should have been grateful for what she'd had when she had it.

Alex had followed them out to the park in a rattly green pickup, parked on their site behind their station wagon, and then proceeded to build the fire, carry water, help Pam put up the tent. He'd even peeled potatoes for supper and dried dishes while Pam had washed. There wasn't a single one of Caitlin's jobs he hadn't taken over.

It wasn't that she would ordinarily object to getting out of helping with dishes, but jobs like that were different when you were camping. As strange as it might seem, they were part of what you came out here to do.

Alex added another log to the fire, which was still burning high. About this time after supper Pam and Caitlin always began to let the fire burn down to coals so they could roast marshmallows after dark.

Caitlin looked around at the towering pines edging their

grassy campsite. They weren't the fat Christmas tree shapes she was accustomed to seeing in yards and parks around the Twin Cities. These were amazingly tall, and they grew so close together that they shut out the sunlight, allowing no branches to grow for most of their height. All those bare, clustered trunks reaching for the sky gave a feeling of enclosure, almost like the secure walls of a house.

Except for the picnic table and fire pit provided by the park, they might have been camping in the wilderness. They were the only ones at this far end of the campground, and on a weekday so early in the summer they would probably continue to have the place to themselves. That is, they'd have it to themselves if Alex ever left. Surely, he wasn't going to stay the night.

Caitlin picked up a pinecone and tossed it in the direction of the fire. It overshot and hit Alex's foot. He jerked and looked around as though he expected some kind of attack. What was wrong with the guy?

Caitlin stood and moved toward the pair, interrupting their murmured conversation. "How about going for a bike ride before it gets dark?" she asked, speaking pointedly only to Pam.

"Alex doesn't have a bike here," Pam replied, as though Caitlin wouldn't have noticed that. "And the park rental station is closed for the night." As Pam spoke, she reached over, almost unconsciously, it seemed, and put a hand on Alex's arm. Her hand looked white, out of place against the springy black hair on his arm. Even so, the gesture was filled with a familiarity so deep that it brought a rush of blood to Caitlin's face.

She stared at her sister's hand. So that's the way it was! How could she have been so dumb?

"Don't give up a ride because of me," Alex protested. "I should be going home, anyway." He sounded sincere, yet he made no attempt to rise. In fact, his hand crept over to cover Pam's as he spoke.

"It's all right," Caitlin told them both, though it wasn't. It wasn't at all. "I'll go by myself." She turned abruptly from the campfire and grabbed her bike from where it leaned against a tree. Throwing one leg over the seat, she stepped down hard on the raised pedal.

She had already reached the gravel loop in front of the campsite when Pam called after her. "Don't go too far. It'll be dark soon, you know."

As if she cares! Caitlin thought as she sped away. As if it wouldn't suit Pam just fine if the little sister she hadn't wanted along anyway left her and her boyfriend alone for a while . . . left them alone forever.

Chapter Three

CAITLIN STOPPED PEDALING and dropped off the bike. How far had she come? Miles, no doubt. The asphalt bicycle path through the forest was so smooth, so gently graded that there was nothing to require a stop . . . or even a thought about turning back.

But as soon as her feet touched the ground, the anger came flooding back. Pam had used her as a cover for her nefarious plans.

Caitlin liked that word, *nefarious*. Evil, sinister, wicked. She liked all kinds of words, but just now it felt good to know exactly the right word to describe her older sister.

How had Pam dared? How had she thought she would get away with it? Had she figured Caitlin was so foolish — or so young — that she wouldn't understand what was going on?

Alex probably had a tent stowed away in that rattly old

truck of his. And, no doubt, Pam intended to slip out in the middle of the night and go sleep with her boyfriend. Funny, that they called *that* sleeping. Well, she didn't have to worry about little "Linnie" being in her way. She didn't have to worry about her sister being around at all. Caitlin wasn't about to go back and interfere with their fun. She would stay in the forest and live off the land, just the way she had suggested earlier.

She looked around. The trees were close on either side of the bicycle path. They seemed more like prison bars than the comforting walls they'd been earlier. The sky — she squinted to examine it more closely — the sky was no longer blue. In fact, the color seemed to have been pulled from it so that the little patch she could see above the feathery treetops was white. No . . . silver. Pewter. It darkened even as she watched.

The green had gone out of the treetops, out of the underbrush, too. Everything around her might have been sketched in different shades of charcoal.

Caitlin drew in her breath. It was growing dark in the forest. Quickly. Did she really want to stay out here alone, so far from the campground? And leave Pam with the tent, the lantern, the cooler filled with food? Did she want to leave Pam alone with Alex, for that matter?

Maybe her sister needed her there whether she knew it herself or not.

Caitlin turned her bike around and began to pedal back as fast as she had come. She would make it without any difficulty. She even had a light on her bike. It was the kind run by a generator, powered by the turning of the wheel. Her father, an engineer always concerned about energy efficiency, had chosen it because it would never need batteries.

After a few moments, she stopped to activate the generator. Using it made pedaling a bit harder, but not enough to slow *her* down. Besides, with the light on, she wouldn't have to hurry so much.

At first the beam made only a dim streak against the shadowy gray of the path. As the night deepened, the thin rays grew more intense, but instead of lighting her way, they seemed only to make the surroundings darker.

At one point, a grove of tall, slender birch replaced the usual pine. The white bark gleamed, almost illuminated the air around her. Caitlin knew she shouldn't stop, that the night would only grow more black, but she couldn't help it. She slowed, then when her light flickered out completely, stepped off the bike.

It was as though she could breathe better in the midst of the lustrous trunks . . . until the mosquitoes descended on her, and then she pushed on again. There was nothing to be gained by standing there, waiting to have her blood sucked away, waiting for the night to swallow her completely.

She had never used her bicycle light in complete darkness before. At home, she was seldom out on her bike at night, and if she was, there were always streetlights on. Now she found that the light her father had thought would be so wonderful was almost more of a problem than a help.

The light's brightness was determined by the speed with which she pedaled. But as the darkness grew more complete so that she became dependent on the beam to see the path, she had to slow down. To pedal as fast as she must to keep the light bright, she was in danger of overriding the short distance she could see and going off the path. At a more reasonable pace, the light dimmed until it was no use at all.

The dark trunks of the pines, the blackness that puddled between them, pressed in on her from each side. When she looked ahead, as far as the beam of light would let her see, the barred darkness closed in entirely so that the path, itself, vanished.

What might be waiting for her at that point where the path disappeared? Bears? They were far enough north to encounter bears here. It occurred to her, too, that while the bears in the state park had probably learned to avoid people during the day, they must consider the place theirs at night. Even the asphalt bicycle path, this intrusion into their world, would be part of their territory.

A bear startled by a girl on a bicycle, a bear surprised in the night, would be pretty dangerous. Maybe even fatal.

How terrible it would be to die so young. The orphan boy who'd died in the fire must have felt that, how it was all too soon. His life over before it had even begun. He'd been only fifteen, they said. Caitlin tried to shrug away the chill that was climbing her spine, and she leaned over the handlebars to peer ahead as far as she could see.

Maybe old people were ready to die when their time came, though it was hard to imagine. Surely, no fifteen-year-old would have been. Even one who was alone in the world. Like she was alone right now.

The darkness had crept closer, had oozed out onto the path and enveloped the bike, her bobbing knees, even her hands on the grips. The front wheel wobbled and the narrow stream of light with it. Without being able to see, she was losing perspective and balance, too. She stopped pedaling and let the bike roll to a teetering stop. The generator ceased its busy whirring against the wheel. The bicycle light faded into nothing. Black nothing. And she was nothing, too.

Caitlin stepped down cautiously. She knew it made no sense, but it felt as though the very ground might disappear from beneath her in the sudden absence of light.

She wanted to scream. She wanted to stand there, gripping the handlebars of her bike, and shout at the top of her lungs. ''Pam. Pam. Come get me!''

But, of course, Pam wouldn't come. Why should she? She had Alex.

Caitlin took a step forward and then another, feeling with each foot along the ground to make sure the path remained solid. As she pushed the bike, the generator whirred again. The light flickered, illuminating nothing. Almost like a much smaller version of the fire that had danced before her in the museum.

How strange that had been! Even if Alex was right about its all being special effects, she still didn't understand why she had been the only one to see it. And it would seem strange, even perverse, for a museum to set up special effects of someone burning!

The faint beam bounced off the barlike trees, one tree exactly like another so there was no way of telling how far she had to go. And then it bounced off something else, something so unexpected that she stopped walking. She didn't choose to stop; her feet simply attached themselves to the asphalt path. The bicycle light went out, and her legs trembled until she thought they would refuse to hold her.

"It's a bit late for a cycle, isn't it?"

She heard the voice with a rush of relief. It was only a boy, standing in the middle of the path. A perfectly ordinary boy.

He was taller than she, but not much, with pale, straight hair and a round face. His long-sleeved white shirt, even the skin of his face and hands, seemed to glow faintly as if by their own light, exactly as the birches had.

"Who?" she stammered. "Who are you?"

"The name's Frank." His voice was gentle, and not even the forest darkness could hide his friendly smile.

Caitlin took a long, trembling breath and loosened the stranglehold she had on her bike.

It was all right. This boy must have come out to search for

her. Maybe Pam had alerted the ranger that she hadn't made it back to camp, and they had all kinds of people out looking for her. That must be what it was.

"I'm not lost," she defended. "It just got dark before I expected it to."

"I know." The boy smiled more broadly. The night obviously wasn't as dark as she had thought, because she could see his face quite distinctly. He was kind of cute, actually. Maybe even cuter than Dennis Blattner. "Would you like me to walk back with you?" he asked.

Caitlin hesitated. He was a stranger, after all. But then there was just one path, and if he was going in her direction, she could hardly command him *not* to accompany her. Besides, why should Pam be the only one to meet a "friend" on this trip?

"I'm at the campground. Site L-11. Do you know where that is?"

"Certainly," he said. And then, bowing from the waist in a quaint, old-fashioned way, he added, "It's not good, you know, a pretty girl like you out by herself at night."

Caitlin could feel the blood rush to her cheeks at the words *pretty girl*. No one had ever called her pretty. Well, her parents, of course, and Pam, a long time ago when Pam still bothered to call her anything, but that didn't count. No *boy* had ever said it before. Dennis Blattner had yet to manage to say anything at all.

They walked in silence for a while, Caitlin searching for

something to say. The generator whirred and the light gave out its wavering beam. "My bicycle light runs off the wheel, you know," she said finally, "and that means you have to ride really fast to be able to see anything and then . . ." She stumbled to a stop. It wasn't that the boy wasn't listening, because he seemed to be, but she was chattering like a magpie. What had this boy said his name was, anyway? Frank? She tried again. "Are you camping in the park, Frank?"

"Nearby," he replied. He wasn't whispering exactly, but his voice was soft, almost airy.

"My name is Caitlin," she told him, realizing she hadn't even thought to introduce herself earlier. It was the least offering she could make in exchange for his walking her back to camp.

He nodded as though he already knew.

"Did they send you? Out to get me, I mean?"

Frank said only, "No one sent me."

That was confusing. There were a thousand questions Caitlin wanted to ask. *How did you know I was out here, then? Or if you didn't know, what were you doing here yourself? Do you always walk in the forest at night?* But there was something about the boy that stopped her. As though her questions were irrelevant, somehow. Or as though she would be plaguing him, like the mosquitoes that whined about her head.

"Aren't the mosquitoes terrible?" she said instead, lifting one hand from the bike to flap them away.

— 29 —

"They don't bother me," he replied serenely.

"You're lucky," she said.

He didn't respond. With another boy, even with Dennis Blattner, she would have found the silence disconcerting. But there was something about Frank — or perhaps it would be that way walking with anyone in the rustling quiet of the night forest — that made his silence seem friendly, almost better than words.

It took no more than ten minutes to come to the end of the bicycle path. She had been closer to camp than she had realized all along. And when they stepped out from beneath the dense canopy of trees, Caitlin looked up at the night sky with a little leap of joy. The stars gleamed like tiny beacons, so much brighter, more distinct than they were in the city. A half-moon silvered the grass and the gravel road into the campground.

How beautiful the world was! How lucky she was to be alive! Caitlin turned, wanting in her rush of relief to offer this boy something, some important piece of herself. Before she had a chance to speak, however, he said, "I thank you, Caitlin. You're going to be a great friend."

She was going to be a great friend! What was he talking about? And why was he thanking *her?* He was the one who had come to the rescue. She had done nothing but follow him back to the campground.

She wanted to say all that, but though it was unlike her to

be at a loss for words, she could find none now. It was as though the night silence had invaded her tongue.

They turned into the loop of L campsites. L-11 was easily distinguished by the still-blazing campfire and the two dark figures sitting beside it, very close. So much for Alex's going home!

Frank stopped abruptly while they were still some distance away.

"Don't you want to meet my sister?" Caitlin asked. "And her *boyfriend*," she added, leaning heavily on the word. That was obviously what Alex was.

But Frank shook his head, already turning away. He said only, "I'll see you tomorrow."

Tomorrow? Caitlin didn't know what to say. "Where?" she called after him. "Where will I see you?" But the dark had already swallowed up all but the faintest glimmer of his white shirt and his pale skin and hair.

Chapter Four

STANDING THERE IN THE GRAVEL ROAD, Caitlin felt suddenly foolish . . . and entirely too bold. Why was it that the only boys she ever got to know were the shy ones? But then, shy or not, this one had said she was "pretty"; he had said she was going to be a "great friend." He had even said he would see her again.

She turned and made her way to the campfire, where she settled silently on the ground next to Pam.

Pam and Alex were still talking, or rather Alex was doing the talking now. About his wanting to be a history major. About the fact that no one in his family could understand how he was going to earn a living from history. "As if making money is the only thing that's important," he said.

Without turning her attention from Alex, Pam put a hand

on Caitlin's arm. "I was beginning to worry about you," she whispered.

Just beginning? When would it have occurred to her to do more than begin?

"I'm going to bed," Caitlin announced when Alex paused for breath. She stood and brushed herself off, whisking away Pam's touch along with the crumbs of dirt from the ground.

"I'll be there in just a few minutes," Pam replied, her attention still focused on Alex. "Alex was just waiting to make sure you got back all right before he went home."

Hoping I wouldn't come back, more likely! Caitlin thought, though it occurred to her that she no longer cared whether Alex stayed or went. If she could have Pam's attention only when *he* wasn't around, she wasn't sure she wanted it at all. Besides, she had her own interests on this trip.

Out loud she said, "That's okay. You don't need to worry about me."

She made the long trip to the washroom alone. Looking for privacy, they had chosen a spot as far from the park facilities as possible. When she returned, pulled on her pajamas in the cramped dark of the tent, and crawled into the double sleeping bag she and Pam always shared, Pam and Alex were still talking by the fire.

Caitlin rolled over onto her side, as far as she could get from the place Pam would occupy if she ever came to bed, and closed her eyes.

Frank. He'd said his name was Frank. And he'd been really nice, helpful. She wouldn't mind seeing him tomorrow. She was certainly glad to have seen him tonight.

Still, she couldn't help wondering. If Pam and Alex hadn't sent anyone out to look for her — and it was clear that they hadn't or they would have been looking themselves — what had this boy been doing in the middle of the forest at night?

*

The thunderstorm crackled and banged outside the fragile skin of their tent. It bent the trees until they groaned. And it brought Caitlin upright, her heart pounding.

When she felt Pam's hand on her shoulder, she suppressed a startled jerk.

"Scared?" Pam asked.

"No." Caitlin busied herself dropping the tent flaps against the first spatters of rain. "Just closing the tent so we don't get wet."

Pam turned on her side, her knees crooked, and opened her arms for Caitlin. "Come snuggle," she said. "It's getting cool."

Caitlin hesitated, but only for a second, before lying down again, folding herself into her sister's lap.

"Just like old times," Pam murmured, her arm around Caitlin's waist.

Caitlin didn't reply. Was it like old times? Somehow she

doubted it. Still, she lay quietly, letting the warmth of her sister's body seep into her own.

"Shall we rent a canoe tomorrow?" Pam asked after a time. "Paddle down the St. Croix River? The outfitters will pick us up and bring us back." A drumroll of thunder accentuated the question.

"Just you and me?" Caitlin asked when the thunder had died.

It was Pam's turn to be silent. "I thought Alex would come, too," she said finally. "He's never been before. He wants to try it."

Alex had never been canoeing? But he lived in the middle of canoeing country. At least if he didn't know anything about canoes, he wouldn't expect to run things the way guys so often did.

"I suppose he'll be the duffer, then," Caitlin said carefully. The duffer was the person who sat on his duff in the middle of the canoe, the one who got a free ride.

"Oh, no." Pam sounded shocked. Apparently, the idea of Alex as duffer was unthinkable. "He wants to paddle so he can learn how. We thought we'd make *you* queen for the day."

Caitlin snorted, stiffening so that she no longer fit into the curve of her sister's body. *Queen for the day!* It was a bad joke. She liked to paddle, and Pam knew it.

"Linnie . . . ," Pam said. She seemed to be pleading.

"Caitlin," Caitlin corrected, though she felt ugly saying it. Linnie had always been Pam's pet name for her.

"Caitlin," Pam repeated. She held Caitlin more tightly, preventing her from pulling away, but her tone was stiffer now. "You'll understand someday. I promise."

"Understand what? Lying to Mom and Dad? You could have just told them you wanted to meet Alex. Then you wouldn't have had to bother to haul me along at all."

Pam lay very still for a moment, apparently processing the accusation. "I did tell them," she said finally. "Why wouldn't I have?"

Caitlin jerked away this time, sitting upright again so that the sleeping bag peeled back from Pam as well as herself. "Yeah. Sure. I'll bet you did! And what did Mom say?"

"She said it was fine, especially since you were going to be here, too." She reached up and tugged playfully on Caitlin's pajama top. "You may not realize it, little sis, but you're the chaperon on this trip."

"Then why didn't you tell me? You didn't say one thing about Alex. You never even told me he existed." It was what made this so hard, what made her feel so mean, that Pam had lied to her about what they were going to do.

"I did tell you! I talked about Alex the whole way up! Remember? For one thing I said he told me we should see the museum."

Caitlin opened her mouth to reply, then closed it again.

Pam was probably right. She had said something about someone recommending the museum, and Caitlin hadn't paid much attention. Ever since Pam had gotten home, she'd been talking about people no one in the family knew. Caitlin had quit trying to sort them out.

"Still," Caitlin said, the confidence of her anger beginning to waver, "you didn't tell me he was going to be here . . . with us. I would have heard if you'd said that. And when he showed up, you acted like you were surprised."

Pam sighed. "You're right," she said. "I didn't tell you that." She sounded defeated, but she said nothing more, as though the admission were all that was needed . . . or deserved.

"Why didn't you?" Caitlin persisted.

"I don't know. It just seemed . . . easier, somehow. I'm sorry. I should have told you. I guess I was afraid if I did you might decide not to come, and then Mom wouldn't have wanted me to come either."

So Pam needed her. Caitlin couldn't help being pleased at the admission.

"Besides," Pam added, "you and I haven't had much time together since I went to college. I guess I figured this way I could kill two birds with one stone."

Caitlin winced at the image. She couldn't help wondering how the other "bird" felt. Probably Alex didn't like having a third person here any more than she did.

The thunder crashed overhead, and a sudden white light penetrated the walls of the tent. As though a cloud had been ripped open, the rain came against the thin nylon in a pounding rush.

Pam touched her back, and Caitlin lay down once more.

"It does change things," Pam admitted, "having Alex here. I know that. But someday you'll have a boyfriend, too, then you'll under — "

"I already have one," Caitlin interrupted, her irritation growing at Pam's condescending tone.

"A boyfriend?" Pam sounded surprised, almost too surprised. She sounded, oddly enough, very much like their mother had the time Caitlin tried to talk to her about Dennis Blattner. "What's his name?"

"Frank," Caitlin found herself saying, though the name, even as it fell from her lips, surprised her.

She expected Pam to ask her a million questions at least. Where did you meet him? (In the forest . . . on my way to grandmother's house.) What's his name? (Just Frank.) How old is he? (Who knows?) What do his parents do? (Would Pam ask that?)

However, she didn't ask anything. She just said, in a considering kind of way, "Well, that's nice, I guess." She yawned and drew Caitlin close again in the warm, slightly musty-smelling sleeping bag. "Then you should understand already."

"I suppose I should," Caitlin replied, though she didn't. She didn't even want to understand.

For a long time, Caitlin lay very still, listening to the storm rattle and boom. Pam had gone back to sleep almost immediately, as though something had been settled between them. Each exhaled breath tickled the back of Caitlin's neck.

But nothing was settled. Maybe, Caitlin thought, if she hadn't been lying when she'd said that about having a boyfriend, Pam's explanation would be enough. But, of course, it was a lie.

Dennis Blattner didn't count. And Frank . . . well, Frank, at least, had spoken to her. If she were being melodramatic she might even say that he had come to her rescue when she was in distress. But he didn't count either. Not really.

She didn't know anything about him, not even his last name or where he lived. And when he'd said he would see her tomorrow . . . well, sometimes people used words without meaning what they said. *I'll see you tomorrow* was probably just his way of saying good-bye.

All of which left her here, playing chaperon. Playing duffer. The idea that Pam might not have planned this trip except to see Alex, might not have invited Caitlin except to get their mother's permission to be here with Alex, made her like him even less.

He didn't even know how to paddle a canoe, for heaven's sake! Yet he was going to be paddling tomorrow, and she, who had been paddling canoes since she was eight years old, would have to sit there in the middle like some useless little kid who didn't know anything.

Pam turned over in her sleep, releasing her hold on Caitlin's waist. Caitlin flopped over onto her stomach, then turned to her back. The thunderstorm was grumbling away in the distance. A sporadic breeze shook the leaves overhead, sending the last flurries of drops pattering onto the tent. After a while, Caitlin sat up and opened the flap again. The air smelled of pine needles and of wet, black earth. She breathed deeply.

Where was Frank now? When she'd asked if he was camping here in the park, he'd said he was "nearby." But where would "nearby" be if he wasn't in the campground?

It had been considerate of him to walk her back. Not that she'd been lost or anything like that. In fact, it had been rather embarrassing to see how much lighter everything had begun to look the moment Frank had shown up. It just proved how your mind played tricks on you, especially when you let yourself get a little spooked.

He'd said she was pretty. She lay down again, shaking her head. What good did it do to meet an interesting boy in a state park a hundred miles from home?

Whatever he'd said to her, however much he might seem to like her, she was probably never going to see him again.

Chapter Five

THE CANOE SKIMMED THROUGH THE WATER as though being drawn by an invisible string. Alex was in the bow; Pam, in the steering position in the stern; Caitlin, of course, in the "duffer's" seat in the middle. She sat hunched over, her elbows resting on her knees, glowering at Alex's back.

Either he'd been lying about never having been in a canoe — which is what she suspected — or he was a lot more athletic than he looked. Whatever the reason, he seemed relaxed and confident. He paddled with ease and adjusted to Pam's commands almost before she could utter them.

Caitlin had tried a few times to rock the canoe to see if she could get Alex to react, but he had gone on paddling as though nothing were happening at all. Perhaps he didn't realize how easily a canoe could go over. About the third time

Caitlin had leaned to one side, making the canoe lean, too, Pam had said sharply, "Caitlin, stop it!" And she had stopped.

She tried to rejoice inwardly over the fact that Pam had remembered to call her Caitlin, but there hadn't been much joy in that particular victory. She'd always liked the nickname Linnie. Besides, except for that one scolding, Pam didn't call her anything at all. She might have been the invisible girl.

Pam and Alex talked back and forth to one another as though the space between them in the canoe were empty. There was certainly nothing difficult about paddling a canoe down a quiet patch of river, but Pam kept complimenting Alex on how well he was doing. His strokes were "so smooth," she said, "so efficient." And the two of them exclaimed softly over every deer that appeared on the riverbank, every fish that flung itself into the air and plopped into the water again.

Caitlin shifted on the hard metal seat and loosened the straps of her life vest. Her "duff" was getting sore, and the life vest made her feel like a piece of salami between two slices of bread. For some reason, when she was paddling she had never noticed how uncomfortable a canoe could be.

The same way she had never noticed how little her sister really cared about her.

Pam hadn't believed her about seeing the fire in the museum. Even if the whole thing had been done by some kind of special effects, Pam shouldn't have doubted her. And her sister hadn't bothered to ask how she had gotten back to their campsite the night before, whether she'd been lost or perhaps a little scared. She hadn't even been interested enough to ask for any details about the "boyfriend" Caitlin had named.

Thinking about Frank set Caitlin wondering if she had thanked him for walking her back. Things had happened so fast once they had reached the campground that she couldn't remember what she had said.

Another fish jumped between the canoe and the near bank. She didn't see the fish. She heard the sharp plop and watched the circles widen in the water.

She wished air were like water, that when you moved through it you could leave a wake behind . . . one people could see. Then even if they didn't notice you, they would have to be aware that you had been there. Or you could set up enough commotion to make them aware.

Frank had noticed her. He had been more concerned about her being alone in the night forest than Pam had been. He had — Caitlin stared toward the tangle of leaves that grew down to the shore. She stared and blinked and stared again, amazed.

There was Frank standing on the riverbank as though she had called him up by thinking about him! The blond hair. The round face. The white, long-sleeved shirt. He was peering out from behind a bush, not twenty feet ahead of them on the right bank.

But then, before Caitlin could think or speak or lift a hand to wave, he was gone. He looked straight at her, nodded, and stepped back. The heavy foliage swallowed him up exactly the way the darkness had the night before.

Caitlin leaned forward, willing the bushes to part again so she could see the boy behind them. Surely this wasn't what he had meant by seeing her today. And if it was, how had he known she was going to be out on the river, anyway?

As they moved on, Caitlin turned to examine the bank. There was nothing to be seen but the dense, almost impenetrable network of green.

"Look at the turtle sunning on the log," Pam called to Alex.

"A pretty good life if you ask me," he replied, though no one had asked him.

Caitlin didn't know why the exchange annoyed her, but it did. There was very little talk that didn't sound ridiculous — or boring or dumb — if you weren't interested in the topic or the people speaking. She had discovered that listening in on conversations between strangers on the city bus. But she couldn't help noticing that everything Pam or Alex said seemed particularly inane.

She liked that word, too. *Inane.* If she ever saw Frank again, she was sure they would find something better to talk about than "the good life" of turtles.

And then, there he was again. Standing boldly on the edge of the river this time. The surprise wasn't so much that he could move along the bank as fast as Pam and Alex were paddling — it wouldn't be all that difficult to do — but that he would want to.

Caitlin lifted one hand to wave. More of a casual salute than a wave, actually. She didn't want to seem like some too-enthusiastic little kid. After all, it wasn't exactly the first time a boy had been interested in her.

If *interested* was the right word for what was going on.

But Frank waved back enthusiastically, and Caitlin turned to extend her vague salute into a real one. Too late. He was gone again.

Pam gave her an inquiring look. She seemed to have no idea who Caitlin might be waving at, and Caitlin didn't explain. If her sister couldn't see someone standing right out on the bank . . . well, that was her problem. Surely Alex had seen Frank, though. Maybe, being from around here himself, he even knew him. Caitlin held her breath, waiting to see if Alex would say something.

But Alex said nothing more than, "There's an island coming up. Let's go by on the left side."

"Sure," Pam replied, altering course slightly.

Caitlin, intent on the right bank where Frank had appeared, wanted to say, "No! Stay to the right!" But if she did that, she would have to explain her reasons, so she bit her lower lip and said nothing.

If Frank decided to appear again, he would have to wait until they came out on the other side of the island. Unless there was a way across between the shore and the island that she didn't know about, a spit of sand, perhaps. Or unless he waded. In most places, the St. Croix wasn't very deep.

It was hard to figure what Frank intended, popping up this way. And it wasn't that she really expected him to show up again, but then, of course, she hadn't expected him to show up the first time, and he had.

She studied the island shore intently, noting every rustling leaf, peering through each break in the foliage.

And then, there he was once more. Not on the riverbank this time, but right out in front of the canoe, standing in the water, on top of the water, actually. There must have been a submerged rock supporting him, of course, but still, it looked quite odd.

Caitlin could only stare. No one had ever liked her *this* much before! She waited for one of the others to react. They could hardly miss seeing someone they were about to bump into.

But Alex had turned around from the bow to say something earnest to Pam about "the end of civilization as we know it," and the two of them were, as usual, looking at nothing except each other.

Frank smiled, lifted one hand to doff an imaginary cap the way a little old man might do, and said calmly, "Hello, Caitlin."

"Watch out! We're going to hit him!" Caitlin cried. And though she knew better, had practically been born knowing better, she lurched to her feet, pointing.

— 46 —

The canoe rocked from side to side — once, twice — and Caitlin struggled to keep her balance. The struggle didn't last long though, because the next thing she knew she was stretched, flat out, in the stunningly cold water. Pam and Alex were in the water, too, making a great commotion. And the canoe had capsized.

A paddle floated past Caitlin's nose before she could right herself to grab it. The paddle was followed by a small styrofoam cooler she knew to be full of Pepsi. She managed to stand up — the water, she discovered, wasn't more than hip deep here — and grab the cooler.

Pam hung onto the upside-down canoe, and Alex waded after her paddle, still holding his own. Caitlin turned toward the spot where Frank had been standing. There was no one there. She couldn't even make out the rock he must have been standing on.

She looked then toward the maze of foliage along the edge of the island. The shore was only a few feet away from where Frank had been standing. He could have jumped into the bushes pretty fast. But what was the point of going around appearing and disappearing like that, anyway?

"Why did you do that, Caitlin?" Pam was as angry as Caitlin had ever seen her. "You know better than to stand up in a canoe."

Caitlin studied Pam's face. Was she playing games? "Didn't you see? He was practically in front of us! We were going to hit him for sure."

"Who?" Alex asked. He had waded up to them, carrying the paddles.

Caitlin looked to her sister for help. Maybe Alex hadn't seen — he'd been turned in his seat — but Pam must have. There was no way she could have missed someone standing right out in front of the canoe that way.

But Pam just stood there in the cold water, waiting for Caitlin to answer. It was obvious she had seen nothing.

Caitlin's teeth were beginning to chatter, and not entirely from the river chill. "It was him," she said, knowing, somehow, that her explanation wasn't going to help. "Frank. The boy I was telling you about. Only I didn't really tell you, because you didn't ask."

Behind her, Alex made a choking sound, as though he had only now gotten around to clearing his throat of water from the spill, and Caitlin turned desperately back to him. Surely he must know something about what was going on.

If he did, he revealed nothing. He just stood there, the water lapping around his thighs, obviously astonished and yet, somehow, tightly closed at the same time.

Caitlin caught the look Pam was sending Alex — the kind adults passed over the head of an awkward child. It was embarrassed, apologetic, as if *she,* Caitlin, were the one who was behaving oddly. It was exactly the same look she had passed him when Caitlin was describing the fire she'd seen in the theater.

"Where is he now, Caitlin? Can you show us where he went?" Pam spoke with a careful patience that wasn't patient at all.

But, of course, Caitlin couldn't show them anything of the kind.

Pam's cheeks were flushed; her blue eyes blazed. "Neither Alex nor I saw anyone," she pointed out, still with that icy calm that was worse, somehow, than shouting. "I don't know why you —"

"Never mind," Caitlin interrupted. "It doesn't matter." It did, of course, but it was clear, as it had been in the museum, that if Alex and Pam hadn't seen anything, she wasn't allowed to see anything either.

Which didn't change the facts. She had seen Frank, and she was beginning to suspect that, whether she wanted to or not, she would see him again.

The next time he turned up, though, he was going to have a few things to explain!

Chapter Six

CAITLIN COULDN'T STAND IT ANY LONGER. They had canoed to their pickup point in a sodden silence, and the silence had followed them back in the outfitter's van. Now they had been at their campsite for at least half an hour — Alex had built up the fire again, of course — and Pam had yet to say two words to her.

"I'm going for a ride," Caitlin said finally, taking up her bicycle.

Pam shrugged. She still didn't speak.

It was Alex who laid a restraining hand on the handlebar of the bike. "Where are you going?" he asked, as if it were any of his concern.

"Just along the bike path." Caitlin wanted to jerk her bicycle from his grasp, but she didn't. There was no sense in making Pam angrier still.

Alex released his hold, one long finger at a time, studying Caitlin as he did. But he said only, "Don't go too far."

Caitlin sniffed. "I got back last night, didn't I?"

"But it was pretty dark," he pointed out. "We were getting worried."

Had they been worried? Really? Caitlin wanted to ask, but she didn't. She just climbed onto the bike.

As she pedaled away, she knew they were both watching. The skin just between her shoulder blades seemed to bunch under the pressure of their gaze. She thought of turning back, apologizing to Pam, maybe even to Alex, but what was there to apologize for, anyway? For seeing things they were too wrapped up in each other to notice?

Turning onto the shadowy forest path, she found herself thinking, *Maybe I'll see Frank again.* And then she surprised herself by shivering, her skin sweaty and cold at the same time. But there was nothing to be afraid of. She reminded herself of that. Even if she did see him again, he was just a boy, a boy who liked walking in the night forest, a boy who played disappearing games along the riverbank.

Caitlin's parents and teachers had always said she was "an imaginative child" — which wasn't meant as a compliment, she knew — but she had never been inclined to see things that didn't exist before now. Surely her imagination wasn't good enough to call up either fires or boys that weren't really there.

Frank had been as solid as the bike she was riding on. She was certain of that. Maybe if she found him again, he'd be able to explain what was going on. The problem was, of course, where to begin looking. The only solution she could think of was to go back to the place they'd met the night before. If she was there, maybe he would find her. She pedaled steadily on.

In the daylight, she rode through a dreamy, dappled light. Small animals, probably ground squirrels, rustled through the undergrowth. Bird voices drifted down from the distant tops of the trees. The bicycle hummed along the asphalt path. For every rise that caused her to pedal harder, a decline followed that allowed her to coast.

Where had she been the night before when she and Frank had met? It was hard to decide. The forest looked entirely different in the light.

When she came to a clearing, she slowed and let her bike coast to a stop. This would be as good a place as any, she supposed. At least she would be out in the open so he couldn't sneak up on her the way he seemed to have a habit of doing.

She wheeled the bike off the path and propped it against a tree, then looked for a place to sit. She found nothing. There would probably be chiggers in the grass, anyway. Or ticks. And, of course, there were mosquitoes everywhere.

She flapped a hand in front of her face, trying uselessly to clear a path through the whining pests. Did forest fires kill mosquitoes along with the animals and people? If so, that would be one good thing it did.

The people caught in the fire wouldn't care what it was doing to the mosquitoes, though. Like that boy, for instance, the orphan who'd been left behind at the mill.

"I thought you'd come," a voice said from immediately in back of her.

Caitlin jolted in surprise, her teeth even clacking together. She wheeled around. It was Frank, of course, and though she had come hoping to see him, she couldn't help but be annoyed at the way he'd startled her again. He must think it was funny to be always popping up suddenly in unexpected places.

"You seem to be the one coming after me," she pointed out, reasonably enough. "I'm just off for a ride on my bike."

"But you were thinking about me. You were waiting for me to show up." He was actually smirking.

Caitlin couldn't help being annoyed. "If you must know, I wasn't thinking one thing about you. I was thinking about something that happened a long time ago, about somebody from then, too."

"Who?" Frank asked. His eyes were positively sparkling with pleasure at this game, whatever it was, he thought they were playing.

"You probably wouldn't know anything about him," she

replied, a bit more haughtily than she had intended. The boy was so irritating. It made it worse that she had come out here hoping to see him, exactly as he had said.

Now that she looked at him closely for the first time, she saw that he was rather oddly dressed. He was wearing suspenders, for one thing, and his shirt was too large, collarless, and made of some kind of rough fabric. His dark pants were pretty shapeless, too.

She hadn't realized that country kids dressed so strangely.

"You were thinking about the orphan," Frank said cheerfully. "The one who burned up in the fire. Same as when I met you last night."

Caitlin was stunned. That *was* what she had been thinking about, of course! But she wasn't pleased to have her mind read. She had seen people do those kinds of tricks on television, but no one had ever done it to her. She felt curiously invaded.

"How . . . how do you know?" she stammered. Then she added, in an effort to reestablish some kind of control in this conversation, "And even if I was, a little bit ago you said I was thinking about you."

"That *is* me," he answered, and he actually tucked his thumbs behind his suspenders and pulled the suspenders out, apparently to make room for his chest to swell.

Caitlin laughed. This had to be some kind of a joke. "Come on," she said. "I'm not exactly dumb."

"Who said you were?" He studied her seriously as though

her "dumbness" might be an interesting topic of conversation, but his brown eyes were still bright with mischief.

Exasperated, she shook her head. And to think that she had referred to Frank as her "boyfriend." The kid was positively weird! "That boy's dead," she said, feeling foolish for even bothering to explain. "He's been dead for a hundred years."

"So?" Frank cocked his head to one side and thrust his hands deeply into his pockets.

"So you can't be him."

Frank's face fell. He seemed dismayed to have been found out in his silly game. "Who am I, then?" he asked. He was pretending to be serious, even sincere, but the corners of his mouth tweaked in a most annoying manner.

"How should I know?" she cried. She hadn't meant to let him get to her. She knew boys like this one. They liked nothing better than to stir people up. "You tell me."

"I just did."

"Sure." Caitlin rolled her eyes and turned away. She didn't need such foolishness. She walked over to where she had left her bike.

Why had she come looking for Frank, anyway? So he had some secret paths along the banks of the St. Croix and a pretty slick system set up for appearing and disappearing. What was that to her? The next time he decided to perform for her she wouldn't flip any canoes over it.

She picked up her bike and turned to confront him one

last time. "You're really weird, you know that? Anybody who goes around pretending that he's a . . . a . . ." The word caught in her throat.

"A ghost?" Frank supplied, his round face all gleeful innocence.

"Yeah. Anybody who goes around pretending that is full-scale nuts!" She circled a finger at her temple to emphasize her point.

It was proof of how strange the boy really was that his expression never changed. He didn't get angry or hurt or even quit smiling. He just stood there, his hands in the pockets of those country-bumpkin pants, obviously perfectly content with himself.

She lined up the bike. "Out of my way," she said roughly. Frank was standing in the exact center of the bike path. "I'm going back to my campsite."

He didn't budge. His expression didn't change, either. He simply stood there, smiling that teasing, superior kind of smile that made her want to give him a good punch. Not that she usually went around getting into fights.

"Move," she commanded, more loudly than before, and she mounted her bike.

Frank stood firm, his feet spread, his hands still stuffed casually into his pockets in a posture of total unconcern.

She could have ridden around him by going off the path on one side or the other. He was a good twenty feet away from her, and it would have been easy enough to do. Or she could even have ridden on in the other direction for a while longer. By the time she returned, he would certainly have grown tired of standing there and have gone off . . . wherever it was he went. However, she didn't intend to do either. There seemed to be a principle at stake here, though Caitlin couldn't have said exactly what it was.

It had to do with Frank's having made a fool of her on the river, getting her to stand up and tip the canoe, disappearing when she tried to tell Pam and Alex about him. It had to do, too, with this disgusting game he was playing, pretending to be a ghost, even worse, pretending to be the ghost of that poor orphan boy who'd died in the Hinckley fire.

She mounted the bike. "It's your last chance," she warned, aiming for the middle of the path, which was also the middle of Frank. "Get out of my way!"

Frank's smile didn't flicker. He looked maddeningly confident, standing there.

Well, Caitlin decided, if he wanted to play chicken, he'd better be prepared to be the chicken. Because she'd had enough. She stepped down on the pedal, and the bike surged forward. Then she pressed down on the other pedal, picking up speed.

Until the last instant, she was certain Frank would dive for the long grass beside the path, that his impervious expression was all a sham. Any sane person would. He probably thought she would turn aside just because she was a girl, but he would be ready to protect himself in case he was wrong. After all, in a collision, he was the one at the greatest risk.

It was only in that absolutely final, too-late-to-change-her-mind second that Caitlin realized how wrong she had been. That was just before her front wheel blasted through the standing figure, dissolving it, sending it swirling off in every direction like mist in a gust of wind.

She cried out and closed her eyes. Something brushed against her face, something cool, slightly silky, and smelling distinctly of smoke.

Chapter Seven

CAITLIN SQUEEZED THE BRAKES, HARD, and the bicycle came to such a sudden stop that she was nearly thrown over the handlebars. She dropped to the ground and stood there, gasping for breath, her eyes still shut tight, leaning her full weight on the bike.

What had happened? What could it have possibly been?

It wasn't, it couldn't have been what it seemed. She was a *reasonable*, intelligent, thirteen-year-old girl. Living in the state of Minnesota. In the United States of America. In the last decade of the twentieth century. She didn't believe in ghosts.

Nobody she knew believed in ghosts. Not really. Well, kids liked to scare one another with tales sometimes, but everyone understood they weren't real. Like movies about space invaders or vampires.

Slowly, carefully, she turned back to where Frank had been standing. There was nothing. Nothing at all. No cocky boy. Not even the scattered remains of one. She was alone in the buzzing afternoon forest.

She shuddered. Her skin prickled, and the fine hairs rose along her arms. So Frank was exactly what he had said. Even having blasted through him with her bike as she had, she could hardly get her brain to comprehend the idea.

Gathering her strength, she climbed back onto her bike and began to pedal rather unsteadily toward the campground. As the bicycle tires sang on the asphalt, she stared intently at the few inches of path immediately before her front wheel. That path was solid, real. There was nothing more she wanted to see. If she could have closed her eyes and found her way without seeing that, she would have gladly done so.

What would she do if Frank appeared again? Scream? Faint? She had never fainted in her life, and she had always thought old-fashioned stories in which girls and women fainted were silly. If she had to face the ghost again, though, she wouldn't mind being able to pull off a good faint. It seemed as sensible a response as any.

When she emerged from the forest onto the gravel lane of the campground, she increased her speed. Curiously, she felt more vulnerable away from the trees. Even the breeze that reached her here made the skin tighten on the back of her neck, as though she were being breathed on by a thousand ghosts. For a few seconds after she jumped from her bike in front of L-11, she thought her legs weren't going to hold her, but then they did . . . barely.

Alex was squatting over the fire pit, tending another fire. He seemed to need to keep one going every minute. When Caitlin and Pam were alone, they didn't usually start a fire at all until evening unless they needed it for cooking. He jumped to his feet when he saw Caitlin, his eyes intent on her face. "Is something wrong?" he asked.

"I saw . . . I saw . . . " Caitlin stammered, but then she stopped, unable to get the rest out.

"What?" Pam looked up from the food she was preparing, her expression sharp, skeptical. She didn't move.

"Who?" Alex asked. He stood there, alert and wary, scanning the edge of the forest.

Caitlin stared first at one, then at the other. Pam was ready to be angry all over again. Alex seemed . . . It was hard to define. He looked almost guilty, as though he expected to be accused of something, though what it might be Caitlin couldn't imagine.

"Was it a bear?" Alex asked. "Did you come across a bear in the forest?" There was something about the way he said it that seemed to beg her to agree.

"No . . . it was a . . . " But before she could get the word *ghost* out, Caitlin caught the look in her sister's eyes. If Pam was upset about the fire, angry about her turning over the canoe, what would she do if Caitlin announced she'd just seen a ghost?

Caitlin swallowed, hard. "Yes, a bear," she said instead, the lie coming out in a hoarse whisper. "That must be what it was."

Pam and Alex nodded simultaneously. They seemed, each of them, relieved. Only a bear. Nothing strange about that. Everyone knew there were bears in the forests in northern Minnesota.

"Bears can be awfully scary." Alex spoke in a "grown-up" voice that made Caitlin squirm. A tone like that was bad enough coming from a real adult. "Especially when you come across one unexpectedly. But black bears rarely bother people. They'll run if you make enough noise."

"How big was it?" Pam asked, apparently ready to be friendly now that she knew Caitlin wasn't going to cause more trouble.

"Oh . . . it was big," Caitlin answered. "Real big." And she reached to hold her hand just above her head, as tall as a boy — the ghost of a boy, actually — one might meet on the path. Alex looked skeptical, even amused, so she reconsidered. How big were bears, anyway? She held her hand lower, about three feet off the ground.

"Standing?" he asked. "I mean on his hind legs?"

Standing? Caitlin couldn't decide. She nodded.

Alex began to laugh, enormously pleased with himself. "That was just a cub, a yearling." But then he must have noticed something in her expression because he stopped laughing and said, more soberly, "You were right to get out of there just the same. If you saw a cub that size, the mother was probably close at hand. It's best not to take any chances."

Caitlin nodded again, abruptly, but it was hard to let the matter drop. As she wheeled her bike past Alex to put it away, she mumbled, "This one didn't have a mother. He was an orphan."

She hadn't meant anything by it, really. It was just something to say, a small piece of the truth she didn't dare reveal. But to her surprise, Alex snapped to attention as though she had poked him with a stick.

She eyed him carefully as she propped her bike against a tree, wondering what was wrong with him. He said nothing more, though, just turned away and busied himself, again, with the fire.

What would Pam and Alex do if she actually did tell them about Frank? Yell at her for lying? Haul her off to a shrink? But though she knew there was no way she could convince them, there wasn't the slightest question in her own mind about what she had seen. Frank was as *real,* if that was the right word, as any flesh-and-blood person she had ever encountered.

She scanned the edge of the woods. Surely Frank wouldn't

— 63 —

show up here. But she had no idea what she would do if he did. If he walked into their campsite, she would probably be, again, the only one to see him. If she pretended she couldn't see him either, would he go away?

Somehow she doubted whether getting rid of Frank would be quite so easy as that. He seemed a very determined boy. And now that she knew who — what — he was and how easily he could appear, his promise the first night to see her again had begun to feel more like a threat.

Too bad no living boy had ever been so interested in getting to know her.

Pam had gone back to collecting food for supper. She took a package of bratwurst from the cooler. "We'll roast these over the fire," she said, "and we've got a can of pork and beans and cabbage for slaw. But we'll need more water for cleaning up." She indicated the sooty pot they used to heat dishwashing water over the fire pit grate.

Caitlin knew Pam meant for her to get the water, but she turned away, pretending not to understand. She wasn't about to go off anywhere Frank might be waiting for her. Not even to the water spigot just on the other side of the L loop.

Alex came to the rescue. "I'll get it," he said.

"Never mind." Pam was angry all over again, though certainly not at Alex. Her words were clipped. "I need to go to the rest room, anyway. I guess I can do both on the same trip." And without waiting to see whether Caitlin would change her mind — she wouldn't have, anyway — Pam took up the pot and headed off toward the rest room, several loops away.

Caitlin stood where she was in the middle of the campsite, wondering what to do with herself, which way to turn. Somehow she wasn't a whole lot more comfortable being left alone here with Alex than she'd be left behind with the ghost.

There was something strange about her sister's boyfriend. Something that didn't add up. When she had talked about seeing the boy along the river, for instance, he had seemed as surprised as Pam, and yet . . . it was the wrong kind of surprise, somehow. As though he half guessed, maybe even knew what she had seen but just didn't expect *her* to see it.

And just now, when she had come back, he hadn't asked *what* had frightened her, but *who*. Why would he assume she had met a person . . . in the forest . . . with the park being nearly empty of people on this weekday in early June?

Caitlin examined Alex more closely. His face was closed off in that perpetually blank mask. As though he were hiding something. Something, some*one* he was afraid to admit that he knew.

Slowly, her conviction growing, Caitlin moved toward the fire, where Alex was again crouched, poking the burning logs with a stick. She stood there until he was forced to look up. When he did, he smiled at her, but the smile was cautious, even timid.

"You know exactly what's going on, don't you?" she said, not bothering to return the smile. "You know who it was I saw."

Alex didn't answer at first. Instead, he went back to fiddling with the fire. After a moment, he withdrew the stick and examined its smoldering tip. Then he dropped the whole thing into the flames and rose to his full, rather astounding height. "Why don't you tell me?" he said in an ominously hushed voice.

Chapter Eight

"YOU SAW HIM, DIDN'T YOU? On the river this morning." Caitlin held herself still, studying Alex, waiting for a response.

"I didn't see anyone on the river this morning," he replied at last. Then he looked directly at her. "But I think I can guess who you saw."

"Then guess." She kept her voice low, but it was almost an order.

Alex's face remained perfectly impassive. They might have been discussing the weather. "It was him. It was Frank," he said.

Caitlin let out a burst of breath she hadn't known she was holding. "So . . . you've met him, too."

"Did he tell you that?"

She shook her head. "He didn't need to. *You* told me. The

way you've been acting told me." And then in a flash of inspiration she added, "You're keeping the fire going to keep him away, aren't you? He must be afraid of fires . . . considering."

Alex tugged on his beard the way he perpetually did. Instead of answering her question, he replied, "Tell me what you know."

"That he's a ghost." Merely saying the word made Caitlin's skin crawl again. "That he's the boy, the orphan they told about in the museum, the one who died in the Hinckley fire." And then she thought of something that hadn't occurred to her before. "He's the same one I heard calling from the fire in the museum, isn't he? That wasn't special effects at all."

Alex didn't speak. He simply stood there, peering down at her from his great height. Then he turned and walked away. For a moment Caitlin thought he was going to keep on walking, to leave her with her questions . . . and her ghost. But when he got to the picnic table he sat down on the low bench and patted the place beside himself as a signal for her to come sit as well.

When Caitlin did, leaving a careful expanse of wood between them, he said, "You must have been thinking about Frank when you saw him. Right? Here and in the museum, too?"

Caitlin pondered that. She remembered Frank's saying to

her in his cocky way, *But you were thinking about me. You were waiting for me to show up.* And now that she considered it, she supposed she had been thinking about him each time she had seen him. Either about the orphan boy in the film or about Frank, the boy who had helped her out of the forest, not realizing the two were the same.

"Do you have to be thinking about Frank to see him? Is that why you and Pam didn't notice him along the river this morning?"

Alex stared off into the forest. "That's the way it seems to work."

"But you've seen him before, other times, haven't you?"

Alex nodded. "Often. I used to like seeing him. He was almost a friend. But lately . . ." He wrapped his arms around his narrow chest and stopped speaking, letting whatever he had started to say hang there in the air between them.

"Lately what?" Caitlin prompted.

When Alex started up again, however, he was on another track. "You see I'm . . . not an orphan exactly, but my mother was too young and not married. When I was still small, she ran off and left me with relatives to rear. They were all good people, but they had their own kids to worry about. Me, they sort of passed from hand to hand."

Caitlin waited for him to finish. What did any of this have to do with Frank?

"I used to envy my cousins," Alex continued, "because

they each had a peg, a permanent peg to hang their coats on. I never did. I asked for one once, and my aunt, the one I was staying with then, said, 'Never mind, Alex. You won't be here long enough to bother about that.' " He stopped, gave Caitlin a level look as though he were considering something about her, and added, "I think you have to feel a kind of connection with Frank to be able to see him."

Alex's story was a sudden strong light that revealed Caitlin, too, all her "orphaned" feelings because Pam hadn't been paying more attention to her. She could feel her face grow hot under his scrutiny. "I guess I was," she admitted, "feeling a connection, I mean. I felt pretty sorry for him after I heard his story." *And for myself,* she added inwardly, but she didn't say that.

Alex nodded as though he understood. Caitlin suspected that he probably understood more than he let on.

"If I quit feeling . . . like that, then I suppose he'll go away?" she offered tentatively.

"Once you've seen Frank, you don't seem to have much choice about seeing him again." There was a resignation in Alex's voice, a defeat that filled Caitlin with foreboding.

"But if thinking about him is what brings him, then all you have to do if you don't want to see him is *not* think about him. Right?"

Alex laughed, a sharp, unamused bark. "I wish it were that easy. Have you ever tried to *not* think about something, especially a ghost who's just walked into your life?"

The idea took Caitlin's breath away. "Then it's like . . . it's like, once you've met him, you're . . . haunted!"

She hoped, quite fervently, that Alex would contradict her, but he didn't. "Seems to be the case," he said.

Caitlin looked around a bit wildly. "Then where is he now? I'm thinking about him, we're talking about him. So where is he?" She scanned the trees, the undergrowth, the long fingers of shadows reaching into their campsite. There was no blond head, no smiling, round face.

But Alex didn't even bother to look. "Who knows?" he said. "That makes it all the harder to deal with, don't you see? You can't *make* Frank come by thinking about him. But you can't keep him away unless you can *quit* thinking about him, and that's impossible to do."

Now Caitlin wasn't just frightened; she was angry, too. "It's not impossible. It's not! *I* could do it . . . easy!"

Alex said only, "Good luck," his tone making it clear that he thought she didn't have a chance. He leaned over and slapped a mosquito.

For a few moments they sat there, side by side, the mosquitoes humming around them. Finally Caitlin asked, hesitantly, "Does . . . does he scare you?"

Alex turned to look at her. "He didn't at first. Not much, anyway. I was just a kid, and I thought it was pretty neat, having my own private ghost."

"But now?"

"Now . . ." Alex shook his head. "Lately it's been . . . different."

Caitlin studied him intently. "How?"

Alex was suddenly impatient. "I don't know!" He rotated his shoulders as though to slough off her questions. "Maybe I've just outgrown ghost stories . . . that's all."

Caitlin was incredulous. "You're seeing a ghost, you've been seeing him for years, but you've outgrown ghost stories?"

Alex grimaced, apparently agreeing that there wasn't much sense in what he'd said. "It's just that lately he's been pretty . . . desperate. Like he expects me to do something for him, you know? But I don't know what to do."

A shiver ran along the surface of Caitlin's skin. It was what all the old stories said, that ghosts hung around because they wanted something, needed some kind of help. But it was hard to imagine what Alex could possibly do . . . or what she could, for that matter. "Have you asked him . . . what he wants, I mean?"

Alex shook his head. "I guess I'm not sure I'd want to do it — could do it — if I knew. And the truth is, I'm getting pretty tired of having him hanging around."

Caitlin said nothing, but the heat rushed to her face again. It was exactly the way Pam seemed to feel . . . about her.

As though Pam, too, could be called up with a thought,

she appeared again on the far side of the loop. She had stopped at the spigot to fill the blackened pot.

"Well," Caitlin stood up, "at least we can explain it all to Pam so she won't be mad at me anymore. Maybe she can even figure out how to help him."

"Telling Pam won't do any good."

"What?" Caitlin turned back to stare at Alex.

"She won't believe us. Why should she? If I'd told you about Frank before you'd seen him for yourself, would you have believed me?"

Caitlin didn't answer that. She didn't even want to think about it. "With both of us telling her, she won't have a choice," she said. "Besides, if she starts thinking about Frank, she'll probably see him, too."

Alex shook his head. "You're the first one I've known who's seen him, except for me. And you felt a kind of connection. You've said so." He spoke urgently, his eyes intent on the distant figure. "Years ago, I tried to tell a couple of friends, and one of my cousins, too. But they didn't see a thing. Not even when Frank was standing right in front of them. It didn't take them long to decide that I was pretty thoroughly crazy."

"But Pam . . . Pam wouldn't think that."

"Wouldn't she?"

"No!" Caitlin said it emphatically, even more emphatically because she wasn't entirely sure that it was true. Pam

— 73 —

had never been one to put up with much of what she classi-fied as "nonsense." She didn't even like to read ghost stories or watch them in movies or on TV. Still, Caitlin said, willing it to be so, "She won't, Alex."

Alex shook his head harder, a steady back-and-forth movement. "I like Pam a whole lot." A patch of color appeared on his cheekbones, just at the edge of his dark beard. "I think I love her, actually. And I can't . . . I won't take the chance."

Caitlin was stunned. How could he do this to her? "What do you mean . . . *you* won't take the chance?"

"People are uncomfortable with things they can't under-stand, Linnie. Even if she did believe us — and I'm sure she wouldn't, I don't believe myself half the time, not about this — would you want to impose a ghost on her? So he can fol-low her around, too? For the rest of her life? It would hardly be fair."

Fair? Was it fair that Frank was following *her* around? Was it fair that her sister was barely speaking to her when Alex could have explained everything long before now?

On the far side of the loop, Pam had turned off the faucet. She hefted the heavy pot and started slowly toward them.

"Sooner or later," Alex was speaking in a low voice, his words tumbling out rapidly, "she'd be angry . . . at both of us. No, at me. You're her sister, and you're younger. She would blame me."

"You can't dictate what I can say to my own sister." Caitlin started toward the approaching figure. "*I'm* going to tell her, anyway!"

"Caitlin." Alex called softly, and when Caitlin turned back, so exasperated that she could hardly force herself to listen for another second, he said, almost in a whisper, "If you tell her, I'll deny it. Everything I've just said."

Caitlin stood there, speechless. Pam would never believe her if he did that. Never believe in a million years that her little sister had met a ghost. "You couldn't do that!" she cried when she finally found her voice. "You just couldn't!"

"I'm sorry," Alex said, more softly still, "but she's too important to me."

Caitlin closed her eyes, her fury melting into helpless despair. Then she was utterly alone again. Alone.

Except, of course, for the ghost.

Chapter Nine

CAITLIN SAT ON THE GROUND in front of the campfire, contemplating the marshmallow that drooped on the end of her stick.

Alex and Pam sat directly across from her, roasting their own marshmallows, but she avoided looking at either of them. She wouldn't have wanted to look at Alex if he had been the only other living creature remaining on the face of the earth. And though Pam seemed to be letting go of her anger — neither of them had ever been good at holding a grudge — Caitlin found herself evading her, anyway. She had never in her life kept a secret from Pam, and doing so now left her feeling curiously alone . . . as though she weren't so much walling Pam out as walling herself in.

Her marshmallow ballooned, slipped to the end of her stick.

"Linnie! Watch!" Pam cried. "You're going to lose yours!"

Caitlin watched. She watched her marshmallow slide off the stick and drop into the fire. It lay there for a moment as though impervious to the heat, then erupted into vivid blue flame.

"Minus ten!" Pam tossed Caitlin the bag of marshmallows.

Caitlin caught the bag. She nodded, accepting the call. Usually she and Pam competed to see who could roast the best marshmallows, doing them for one another and rating the results on a scale from one to ten. Minus ten was for a marshmallow lost in the fire. One meant it was charred, but still on the stick. A perfect ten was crisp, golden brown on the outside, hot, sweet liquid on the inside.

She set the bag down without opening it.

"Aren't you going to do another?" Pam asked.

Caitlin put her stick aside. "The fire's too hot. You need coals for marshmallows."

It was a jab at Alex, who had continued to build up the fire, even after Pam had suggested that it be allowed to burn down.

"Our fire builder did too good a job," Pam said, giving him a nudge that prompted a strained smile. She didn't seem to notice his discomfort, though. She just smiled back, her face radiant in the fire's glow. Apparently, love wasn't just blind, it was stupid as well.

Caitlin almost felt sorry for Alex. Almost. It must be terrible to be pursued by a ghost for so many years. No wonder he was always peering over his shoulder, building up fires that no one needed. He had said it was impossible to make yourself quit thinking about something, especially a ghost, but it wasn't going to be impossible for her. Her father had always told her, *You can do anything, Linnie, if you want to badly enough*. And she could, too.

She would keep herself busy, that was all. She wouldn't sit around, thinking about ghosts she didn't want to see. She would do things. Like go for a walk . . . right now.

She stood up. "I'll be back in a little while."

Pam's eyebrows went up like flags. "Don't go off now, Linnie. It's much too late to go anywhere by yourself. Look how dark it is."

Caitlin was caught between appreciating her sister's concern — at least she cared — and being annoyed by her tone. Since when had Pam started sounding so much like their mother?

"It's all right," she said. "I'm not a baby, you know."

"But there's no point — " Pam began.

Caitlin interrupted impatiently. "I can go to the washroom, can't I? Do you have any objections if I walk to the washroom by myself?" It wasn't what she had intended, but it would do. Anything was better than sitting here watching Alex's mournful face that made her think continually of Frank.

Pam shrugged, clearly offended all over again. "Do whatever you like," she said, somewhat sullen herself now.

Caitlin shrugged, too. She hadn't meant to annoy Pam. But there would be time to make it up later when she had this . . . this thing out of her life. "I'll be back in a few minutes," she promised, putting on her most pleasant voice.

Pam nodded abruptly, not even seeming to notice the change.

Caitlin gathered the flashlight from the tent, her kit and washcloth and towel from the back of the station wagon, and started off toward the washroom. It was probably just as well if she didn't wait to go later with Pam, anyway. If she found herself alone with her sister, she might blurt out everything, and what good would that do? Caitlin, the liar. Caitlin, the crazy one!

Pam had been right. The night was dark, but the beam of the flashlight was steady, not dim and wavering the way her bicycle light had been. Still, it illuminated little beyond a narrow path for her feet.

Caitlin began humming to herself. As she moved she flashed the light against the surrounding trees and the empty campsites. It wasn't that she was looking for anything. She reminded herself of that. She was just enjoying the night. The rustling leaves. The tree frogs trilling in the darkness. And something else. . . . What could it be?

Footsteps . . . crunching in the gravel? Behind her? She whirled, aiming the light down the road, but there was nothing. She was being silly, anyway. You didn't hear ghosts. At least not this one. He just appeared, whenever he liked.

She couldn't imagine being dead, hanging around on the edge of other people's lives for a hundred years.

How did Frank spend his time when he wasn't with her or Alex? Maybe there were others who could see him, too. Surely a hundred years didn't feel the same for a ghost as it would for a living person. Probably nothing felt the same.

But no. She wasn't going to think about Frank. She had promised herself. Not even the edge of a thought. The only things she might encounter in the campground of St. Croix State Park were bears, raccoons, porcupines . . . or maybe other campers along the road.

There was a light to her left, deep in the trees. Frank had given off a faint light when she'd seen him that first night. But this — she traced it with the beam from her flashlight — was only a tent, a lantern glowing inside. And then, without intending to really, she found herself whirling again, shining the flashlight in a rapid circle that left a blurred trail in the air.

But she wasn't thinking about Frank. She wasn't! She was looking for bears. Or skunks. Skunks were nocturnal, and who wanted to stumble onto one of them in the dark?

The wind rose and died again. She could hear it start up in the distance, like an approaching train or the moan of some invisible beast. Then it was stirring the tops of the trees immediately above her. And then it was gone. Like a whole flock of ghosts passing.

"Stop it!" she commanded herself, speaking out loud. "Just stop!"

Fireflies flashed in the clearings. She had read once that all that blinking was meant to attract a mate. It was strange if you thought about it. Everywhere you looked creatures were calling to one another. *Come to me! Come to me!* She turned her flashlight off and on several times. Blink. Blink, blink, blink. Maybe someone would see and blink back.

Not Frank, though. She wasn't thinking about Frank.

The lid banged off a trash can just a few feet away, and she jerked toward the sound like a puppet pulled by a string. The flashlight flew out of her hand. Frank!

With loose-jointed fingers she scrambled in the gravel for the light, which fortunately hadn't gone out. But when she found it again and turned the beam in the direction of the sound, only a masked raccoon stared back at her from the rim of a garbage can. Its eyes gleamed with reflected light.

Caitlin moved on quickly. She was lucky it hadn't been a bear. They were usually the ones who went after garbage at night. Would a ghost be afraid of bears? Would he be startled by sudden noises the way living people were?

She had to stop this! It was Alex's fault, telling her she'd never be able to forget. The night was filled with invisible life, not death. She wouldn't think about Frank again. Ever.

An owl called from a distant tree. One time when they had been camping she and Pam had actually gotten a conversation going with an owl. Caitlin hooted back.

Silence.

She was within range of the electric lights outside the washroom when the last of her courage slipped away. What if someone — anyone — jumped out at her from the bushes or from behind the corner of the building? Of course, she was thinking about some other camper, no one else. But what if he did?

She ran the last hundred or so yards (the faster she ran, the more pursued she felt) and burst through the door of the women's rest room, grateful for the bright lights and the protective walls. It wasn't that she was afraid, though. Or even that she was thinking about . . . things she shouldn't. All she needed was a little time to collect herself, and then she would be fine.

Two gray-haired women, standing at the row of sinks, eyed Caitlin curiously. She leaned against the door to steady herself and forced a smile. From the long, narrow mirror above the sinks, a wild-eyed girl stared back at her. She looked — even Caitlin had to admit it — a bit crazy.

"Dark out there," she said to the women, trying for a conversational tone.

"It certainly is," one of them agreed. "Living in the city, you forget what night is really like."

They began gathering toothbrushes, soap, and towels.

"Is your site far from here?" Caitlin asked, suddenly reluctant to see them go.

"Just over there," the one who had agreed about the dark replied, indicating the direction opposite the one Caitlin had come from.

"When you're our age, you don't like to be too far from the facilities in the middle of the night," the other one added, chuckling amiably at herself.

Caitlin nodded, pretending to understand, and moved toward the sinks herself.

One of the women looked into her face as they passed, and stopped, her hand on the door handle, to ask, "Are you all right, dear?"

"Oh, yes," Caitlin cried, too enthusiastically. "I'm fine!"

The women, believing her, nodded agreeably and left. The door closed behind them with a solid whump.

Caitlin turned slowly from watching their departure and examined herself in the mirror once more. Her face was dirty. She hadn't taken a shower since she had gotten here, and she wasn't going to take one this evening either. The idea of undressing, even behind a lock in one of the shower stalls, was enough to make her shudder.

Caitlin glanced in the mirror again and pressed her index finger against the tip of her nose, squashing it almost flat. She'd been doing that for years, trying, in vain, to make it grow straight.

Frank had said she was pretty, but then what did she care? Who needed to be pretty for a . . .

Caitlin walked to one of the toilet stalls, opened the door, and then opened her mouth to scream. What came out was a strangled squeak.

Directly in front of her, Frank sat on the edge of the toilet seat, his face stretched into a silly grin.

Chapter Ten

CAITLIN STARED AT THE FIGURE perched on the edge of the toilet. At least Frank wasn't actually *using* the facilities. That was some consolation. (Ghosts probably wouldn't have any reason to need toilets, anyway.) But though she wasn't afraid, his presence — especially here — gave her a jolt.

"Do you believe me now?" he asked, still grinning.

It took Caitlin a few seconds to figure out what he was talking about. Believe him? About what? But then she understood. He wanted to know if she believed that he was a ghost.

"I don't seem to have much choice, do I?" She said it crossly to cover the trembling that had seized her entire body with the first shock of his appearance. And then she added, "Don't you know that this is the *girls'* rest room?"

The grin grew even wider. "You're the one who invited me."

Caitlin felt exactly the way she had the time she'd accidentally poked her finger into an open electric socket. Her limbs seemed loose, almost disconnected from her body.

Frank was right, of course, if thinking about him was the same as inviting him in. However hard she had tried, he'd kept climbing into her head. But she clenched her jaw in order to stop her teeth from chattering and said, with as much authority as she could command, "Just because somebody thinks about you now and then doesn't mean that person wants you around!"

The smile faded. "Don't you like me, then?"

"Like you?" The question annoyed her enough to stop the trembling. "What does liking you have to do with anything?"

Frank didn't seem to have an answer for that, and Caitlin sighed and stepped back from the stall. By this time she had decided against using one of the toilets, anyway. She could get up in the middle of the night like the gray-haired women if it came to that. Besides, she wasn't going to have any boy, ghost or not, hanging around while she did anything so personal. Even if she went to one of the other stalls and closed the door, he could probably float right in over the top. Or see through the wall, maybe. Who knew what a ghost was capable of doing?

She kept backing up until she could feel the cold porcelain

of the sinks behind her again and reached for her kit. She would put off brushing her teeth, too. They wouldn't rot and fall out in just one night.

Frank had followed. In fact, he now stood between her and the door. "You really don't like me?" he asked. He seemed bewildered, hurt, as though the idea were beyond his comprehension.

"It wouldn't do a whole lot of good if I did, would it?" Caitlin pointed out as reasonably as she could. "You'd still be . . ." Somehow she had difficulty finishing the sentence.

"Dead," Frank agreed solemnly.

Caitlin tried to suppress a shudder.

"But," he said, "you've *got* to like me."

"Why?"

"Because if you do, then you'll be willing to help."

It was a statement, but it sounded more like a plea, and Caitlin found herself held by it. So Alex had been right. Frank needed something. And if she didn't help him, who would? Alex had as much as said that he wasn't going to.

"What do you want me to do?" she asked cautiously.

He leaned toward her, intent, urgent. "Let me stay with you, that's all." He reached a pale hand as though to take hold of her arm, and Caitlin drew away. She couldn't help it. The idea of being touched repulsed her. What would that ghostly hand feel like, anyway?

If he noticed her repugnance he gave no sign. "Just keep thinking about me, so I can stay close." He made it seem such a small request. He might have been asking her to accompany him on a walk around the block. "It doesn't happen when I have somebody near."

Caitlin didn't ask *what* doesn't happen. She wasn't sure she wanted to know. "Keep thinking about you? For how long?"

Frank's face glowed like a full moon. "Only as long as you live. After that maybe one of your children or grandchildren will do."

As long as she lived! Her children or grandchildren! Caitlin felt as if she had been dropped into icy water again, exactly the way she'd been on the river that morning. "But . . . but," she gasped, "I can't . . . I mean, my whole life? It's . . . it's too much!"

He was still standing between her and the doorway, and though she knew from her earlier encounter that she could have pushed past (through?) him, she looked around wildly for some kind of rescue. Why didn't Pam come? Or her parents. What were her parents thinking of, anyway, letting her go camping? Surely they must know that terrible things could happen when a kid was left all alone.

"You don't understand. I can't have you around all the time," she stammered. "I have school . . . and friends and . . . and . . . I have to study and practice for track. I'm on the girls' track team, you know."

Frank said nothing.

"And sleep. Every night I have to go to sleep." *And have*

privacy to shower and dress and use the bathroom, she thought, but she didn't add that.

"You don't have to worry about me when you're sleeping," he said, as though that were her only concern. "If you dream about me now and then, I'll be fine."

Caitlin shook her head violently. "It must be somebody else you want. Not me. I mean, I'd like to help. I really would. But I can't. Don't you see?" He didn't look as though he saw anything. She rushed on, the words tumbling over one another. "I'll bet Alex could do it. He'd be glad to. Why don't you check with him?" She almost felt mean, siccing the ghost on Alex, but not mean enough to take it back.

"No!" The answer was emphatic. "All Alex thinks about is Pam. Pam, Pam, Pam. He's got no room for me anymore."

She knew exactly how Frank felt, only for her, of course, it was Pam having no room for anyone except Alex. Still, she tried another tack. "But I thought ghosts always stayed near where they died. I live in Minneapolis, you know. It's a long way from here."

"That doesn't matter," Frank was quick to answer. "I can go anywhere you do. You'd just carry me home in your head."

Caitlin shivered. How could Frank possibly think that she would want to do such a thing? And how was it going to help him if she did? She was sorry for him. She really was. But enough to keep him around for the rest of her life?

"I've got to be getting back," she told him, edging toward

the door. "My sister will be worried." Not that Pam was apt even to be thinking about her, but it was something to say.

To her relief, Frank stepped aside, but then as she passed he said, "There's no need for anyone to worry. I'll stay with you."

Caitlin pushed the door open with spaghetti-limp arms, struggling to stay calm. He was only a boy, after all. Only a dead boy. "You asked if I liked you" — she stepped behind the door and held it between them as though it were some kind of protection — "and I guess I like you well enough. But if you follow me around every minute, I'll get so I don't. It happens, you know, when people are together too much."

It had happened to her and her best friend, Deanna, the time they'd gone on a trip to the Grand Canyon with Deanna's parents. After they'd gotten back, it had been at least three weeks before the two of them had even wanted to talk on the phone again.

"I'd be sorry about that," Frank conceded, and he looked as though he would be, "but as long as I can stay near, I expect everything will work out. If you like me . . . well, that would make it nicer, but it's not entirely necessary."

It was all too much. Caitlin slammed the door and took off toward her campsite at a loping run.

But, of course, a slammed door didn't deter Frank. He followed. Actually, he didn't so much follow as he seemed to spring up again close beside her. She didn't even have to turn her head to see the unnatural glow drifting along next to her as she ran. How could she have thought last night that Frank's skin and shirt were merely reflecting the last of the light like the birches?

"I can't do it," she told him. "No one could. It's not fair to ask me to." And she increased her pace.

But though Caitlin was one of the best runners on the seventh grade girls' track team, she couldn't outrun him. There was no sound except for the thudding crunch of her own feet in the gravel, yet Frank kept pace. And his keeping up so effortlessly made her more frantic still.

"I'll forget you," she panted. "I'll never think of you again. Then you won't be able to follow me . . . home or anywhere else!"

Frank laughed, but the laughter no longer sounded particularly friendly. "You mean your life is so exciting" — his words came out smoothly, unaffected by the pace they were keeping — "that you're going to be able to forget about meeting a ghost?"

It was exactly what Alex had said, that she wouldn't be able to forget, but that didn't make it true. "Just you wait," she told him between heaving breaths. "I'll find myself a boyfriend who'll take up every thought in my brain!"

"Don't worry about that," Frank replied, his voice so close against her ear that it might have come from inside her own head. Though it didn't. She knew it didn't. "Haven't I told you? I'm your boyfriend now."

Chapter Eleven

CAITLIN BURST INTO THE CAMPSITE, gasping. Ordinarily she could keep her wind when she was running, but ordinarily she wasn't being chased by a ghost. She jerked open the back of the station wagon and flung in everything she had been carrying. Then she slammed the gate and whirled to face Frank.

He stood there, perfectly still, waiting, but there was an obstinacy in his spread feet, his crossed arms, even in the faint but persistent glow that emanated from every part. Was it possible? Did he really think he was going to stay with her for the rest of her life? To be her boyfriend, for heaven's sake?

"Go!" she said, shouted, really. "Get out of here! I'm sick of having you around!"

A look of injured amazement crossed Frank's face. He even staggered, as though he'd been shoved, and dropped back a step or two.

His retreat, slight as it was, gave Caitlin courage, and she moved toward him, still shouting. "Just leave, will you? I didn't invite you. No one did! You've got no right to be here!"

Frank's entire image wavered, like mist in a sudden breeze. "Caitlin! Don't!" he pleaded.

But before Caitlin could take back her words — or decide if she wanted to take them back — her attention was caught by Pam. She had been sitting on the ground next to Alex a dozen yards away on the other side of the campfire, and she lurched to her feet as though propelled.

Of course! She would think, must think — what other choice would she have? — that Caitlin was shouting at Alex, telling *him* to go.

Ignoring the troublemaking ghost, ignoring Alex, ignoring everything but Pam, Caitlin rushed to meet her sister. "Pam, please . . . I didn't mean . . . It wasn't what you . . ." But every sentence she began stumbled and stopped unfinished. How could she possibly explain?

Caitlin had never seen her sister so furious. Pam's face was clenched like a fist, and she spoke with an anger all the more terrible for being held tightly in check. "You are, without a doubt, the most immature, rude, self-centered girl I have ever known!"

"Me, self-centered!" Caitlin gasped. And in that moment, every ounce of her disappointment of the past days rose into her throat. "You're the one. You! You never talk about

— 93 —

anybody except yourself, yourself and your friends. And you don't care about anybody else either. Especially not me. You don't care one thing about me!"

Just behind Pam, Alex had risen now, too, and Caitlin wondered if he was going to intervene. Even if he hadn't seen Frank this time, he had to know that she hadn't been shouting at him. He could explain everything to Pam. But coward that he was, he just stood there, pretending to be helpless and pained.

Pam leaned closer. In the half-light from the fire, her features seemed craggy, harsh. Even her beautiful blue eyes had become hostile, dark smudges. "Do you know what it's like," she hissed, "talking to you these days? It's like talking to a wall. It's like talking to a brick! 'Mmmm-hmmm,' you say, but you don't really hear one single thing I say. You're just waiting, every minute, for me to ask about you."

Caitlin caught her breath. Pam was right! She was absolutely right! That was what she was waiting for, what she had been waiting for ever since Pam had gotten home. Still, was it so terrible to want her own sister to listen, the way Pam clearly wanted her to listen as well?

"But . . . but you never asked," she cried. "Not once. It's like you don't want to know anything about me anymore!"

Alex put a hand on Pam's shoulder, but whether his intention was to encourage or interrupt was impossible to tell.

Pam, however, clearly took it as encouragement. She

snugged in closer to him and threw an arm around his waist. Her head came no higher than his shoulder, but the two of them fit together as neatly as the stones in a wall.

From that position, she continued her tirade. "And the moment Alex showed up, you took to imagining things. Fires in the middle of the museum. Boys in the river. Bears in the woods. Anything to make me pay attention to you." Pam was crying. She was actually crying! "And when that didn't work, you just scream at him to go home. Well, if anyone's going to leave here, it should be — "

"Pam," Alex broke in, finally. "Please, don't."

It was what Caitlin wanted to say to him . . . precisely. *Don't stand there pretending to be innocent. Don't act like this has nothing to do with you!*

Even Pam was exasperated by his interruption. She swiped at her nose with the back of her hand, just like a little kid, and turned to confront him. "You don't need to defend her. She knows what she's doing. She knows exactly."

But Alex, instead of explaining further, instead of helping either one of them, had fallen silent again. He stood perfectly still, his head lifted like a listening deer, staring off toward the edge of the forest.

Caitlin reached to touch Pam's arm, but Pam drew back abruptly. Caitlin let her hand drop without having connected.

How had this happened? One little camping trip, her and

Pam's favorite thing in all the world to do together, had spoiled everything. Forever, maybe. The same forever that Frank was going to be following her around, ruining every single day of her life.

"Pam, I'm sorry. It had nothing to do with Alex. It's just . . ." What was it *just?* How could she explain any of it? "I needed you," she concluded lamely. "Didn't you know that?"

"Don't you think I needed you, to hear *me?* Don't you think I needed you to care about *me?*"

But it wasn't the same, was it? Caitlin was going to protest, to explain how she had always counted on her big sister, but a sudden sound from behind stopped the words on her tongue. It was a scream, and it wrapped around her like a tightly coiled rope.

"Help me! Please!" The same voice, the same words she had heard in the museum.

Even Pam went pale and still, as though she had heard something, too, but couldn't quite make out what it was. Alex remained immobilized, staring off over their heads.

When Caitlin spun toward the voice, she already knew what she would see. Fire sprang toward the night sky, a great eruption of flame, a leaping tower of light.

"Come!" a voice cried from inside the conflagration. "You've got to come help me!"

The flames made no sound. Not even any snapping of

wood or crackling of dry pine needles. And they cast no light beyond themselves, gave out no heat. Yet they reached so high that they blotted out everything, even the towering trees. Even the stars. Everything except for the boy they surrounded.

The ghost of a boy and the ghost of a fire, too.

So this was what Frank was afraid of! Left alone, he relived his own death. Left alone, he burned . . . again and again and again.

She could make out hands, reaching, and from the dark hole of a mouth there issued another scream. It was so terrible that Caitlin found herself screaming, too. And running, running.

"Stop!" Alex cried. "Don't! You'll be — "

Pam was calling, too, a wordless wail that increased in intensity as Caitlin approached the fire.

She couldn't listen to either of them. Alex had already made his choice. And Pam . . . Pam didn't understand. Perhaps it would never be possible for her to understand.

"Please!" Frank wailed. "Please!"

And Caitlin flung herself into the ghostly fire, reaching for the familiar round face, the blond hair, the mischievously dark eyes. For an instant she seemed to have hold of something solid. It was almost like gathering a friend into her arms. And then there was nothing, nothing at all.

Except that, finally, the screaming stopped.

Chapter Twelve

"WHAT WAS IT? WHAT?"

Caitlin couldn't answer Pam's questions. She sat in the pine duff at the edge of the woods, hugging her knees against her chest and crying. There was no place even to begin.

Alex knelt beside her. He didn't attempt to explain anything to Pam, either. But he said, putting a large, gentle hand on Caitlin's shoulder, "You're a brave girl, Linnie."

"But did it help? Did it? Will he have to go through it again?" Caitlin smeared the tears with the heels of her hands, leaving her face wetter than before.

"I'm sure it helped," Alex said, rubbing her back gently. "I think you did exactly the right thing. He's been appearing to me lately . . . exactly like that. Only I never knew what to do for him. Or if I knew, I didn't have the courage to try."

"Who?" Pam demanded, looking from one to the other. "What are you two talking about?"

Caitlin didn't reply. Instead, she took a deep breath and gazed at the surrounding forest. The moon had risen above the trees, etching everything in its flat, unreal light so that all the world was composed of shadows. There seemed no place to begin, so instead of trying, she turned back to Alex. "But where is he now? Do you think he's all right?"

Alex smiled. "I have a feeling that Frank is better now than he's been anytime in the last century. You came when he called. That's what he's been needing, I think, for someone to care enough to come."

Pam interrupted again, her tone exasperated now. "Frank? A century? You two have got to tell me what you're talking about!"

"I guess we do," Alex agreed, and Caitlin nodded her solemn approval.

They took turns telling the story.

When they were through, when they had told every part — including Alex's confession that he had known all along what was happening to Caitlin — Pam was silent.

She sat staring at the grass. Alex, waiting for some kind of response, went back to tugging violently on his beard. Caitlin was beginning to feel sorry for him. If Pam didn't say something soon, he might never need to shave again!

"Well," Pam said, finally, looking first at one, then the

other, "*I* didn't see anything. No fire. No boy. But I did hear . . ." She stopped, then shrugged. "I'm not sure what it was. An owl, I thought. Or the death cry of a rabbit."

She fell silent again, and Caitlin held her breath.

"*But,*" she added finally, giving them both her most no-nonsense look, "no ghost has ever appeared to me, and until one does, I'm afraid I'm still going to be pretty skeptical. I just know that *something* must have happened, something that affected both of you."

Alex nodded, smiled. He looked so relieved that Caitlin almost laughed.

Pam turned to Caitlin. "Linnie, you're right about one thing. I haven't been paying attention to you. Maybe I was feeling kind of jealous. I got back and here you were, still the little girl Mom and Dad looked after. Nothing had changed for you."

"But you had been gone all year," Caitlin reminded her. "That was the biggest change of all."

Pam reached out and ran a gentle finger down Caitlin's ski-jump nose.

In response, Caitlin swooped her finger off the jump in Pam's nose, too. It was one of the things that she forgot when Pam was away, that they both shared this "gift" from their mother. Dad called it a pixie nose. He also called it beautiful.

"I'm sorry, too," she said. "I promise I'll listen after this. Even if you want to talk about *him*." She looked meaningfully at Alex, who ducked his head like a shy little boy.

"Well," Pam said, standing and tugging Caitlin to her feet, "if we're going to start talking about Alex, it must be time for him to go home. Don't you think?"

Alex agreed that it was.

*

Caitlin emerged from the tent, blinking in the morning sunlight. "Your boyfriend's back," she called to Pam. "I guess we overslept." Behind her she could hear Pam begin to scramble for clothes.

"Tell her not to hurry," Alex called, climbing out of his truck. "I'll get started on breakfast."

Caitlin didn't bother to pass the message on. Pam would have heard. More evidence to add to the list she had presented last night, all entitled "Wonderful Alex." After listening for a long time, Caitlin decided that if having a serious boyfriend was going to do *that* to a girl's brain, she was in no great hurry to have one.

When Pam crawled out of the tent, still tousled and bleary-eyed, she gave Alex a distant wave that said, *Don't come near me yet,* then she and Caitlin biked to the washroom in a companionable silence.

There was little that needed saying this morning. Just, "Pass the shampoo," from one shower stall to the next and, "Are you ready to go now?"

As they returned to their campsite, Caitlin stopped at the mouth of the bicycle path into the forest. "I'm going for a ride," she said, "just a short one. I'll be back in time for breakfast."

"If you're late," Pam replied in her old, teasing manner, "we'll feed your pancakes and sausages to the nearest ghost."

Caitlin laughed and pedaled on between the trees. She had nothing to worry about. She doubted very much that ghosts ate, which was another thing that must have made the past century unspeakably long for Frank. All the basic activities that gave pleasure and order and meaning to human lives had died with him in the Hinckley fire.

She wanted to check, just to see if Frank was still around. She could sense that something had changed at the moment when she rushed into that ghostly fire, but she had to know exactly what.

She rode until she came to the clearing where they had met before, and then she propped her bike against a tree and walked into the sweet, sun-warmed grass. She stopped there and took a deep breath. She couldn't help being just a bit nervous.

I'm here, Frank, she called inwardly, and almost immediately he materialized. One minute he wasn't there; the next he took shape directly in front of her.

"Hi," Caitlin said, feeling suddenly and inexplicably shy.

"Hi," he echoed. He, too, apparently, at a loss for words. "I want to thank you," he added after an awkward silence, "for saving me."

"Is that what I did?"

He nodded, but then another silence followed, even longer than the one before, until finally Frank said, "I . . . I'm going away now."

"Away?" Caitlin was astonished, all the more astonished to realize that she wasn't entirely relieved. "Where will you go?"

"I don't know." He was serious, but he didn't seem frightened or concerned. "Wherever the others went, I guess. I'll join them." And then he added, "It's because of you that I can, you know."

If it had been a different kind of conversation, Caitlin might have protested. *No, really! I didn't do anything!* she could have said. But there was something in Frank's manner, solemn and joyful at the same time, that stopped her from filling the air with that kind of noise. She waited for him to explain.

"No one ever tried to save me . . . until you," he said.

"They would have come back for you if they could have," Caitlin said, remembering the story of the fire. "I'm sure they wanted to."

"The funny thing," he continued as though she hadn't spoken, "is that I used to think they'd gone and left me behind again . . . even after I'd died. None of the rest are hanging around still."

"And now? What do you think now?"

"That they didn't leave me behind at all. It was me,

hanging on. It was me reliving the fire, too. Remembering. Hating." Frank's dark eyes were steady on hers. "But after you tried to save me, I just . . ." He opened both hands in a gesture of release. "And then I was on my way."

For the first time Caitlin noticed that her companion was growing fainter, less substantial, even as he spoke. Always before he had seemed solid, like any other human being, but now she could see right through him. The shapes of the trees, the grass, the dark surface of the bicycle path showed clearly behind his white shirt, his broad, friendly face.

"But you came back," she reminded him, suddenly not wanting him to go, at least not yet.

"Just to say good-bye," he said, "to you."

"Oh." Caitlin's throat was clogged with unexpected tears. "Well then . . . good-bye. It's been . . ." She couldn't think what it had been, so she left the sentence dangling there between them.

"You know" — Frank's voice was stronger again — "there's something I never did when I was alive, something I might not get a chance to do on the other side . . ." He seemed to be having difficulty finishing his sentences, too.

"Yes?"

He ducked his head, tugged on his suspenders, and released them again. There was no snap. "I never kissed a girl," he whispered in the direction of the ground, "especially a pretty girl like you."

Caitlin was stunned. Her hand came up, and she pressed the back of it to her mouth as though for protection. Did she want to kiss a ghost? Really? But then she remembered how long she, too, had waited for a moment like this. Not as long as Frank, certainly, but long enough.

"Well," she told him, "then I guess this is your chance."

But he still didn't lift his head, just stood there staring at the ground, and Caitlin wondered if he expected her to make the first move. She wasn't sure she was ready for that. She stood perfectly still. She had waited thirteen years. She could wait a few minutes more.

When he looked at her again, finally, his mouth was already puckered softly. He moved toward her.

For a moment Caitlin could see the fine, blond hairs on his upper lip, just the softest beginnings of a moustache that would never have a chance to grow. And then her eyes were closed, and something cool and soft, something tasting distinctly of smoke, touched her lips.

The kiss was so gentle it might almost not have happened, except that it did.

When Caitlin opened her eyes again, Frank was gone. She waited for a few moments, thinking about him intently, but he didn't reappear. Then she walked slowly to the edge of the clearing, where she retrieved her bike.

Astride the bike, Caitlin paused to look up and down the path, around the clearing, into the fragrant, green forest. A

mosquito whined near her ear. She waved her hand in the air
to drive it away, but it only moved in closer.

She remembered Frank's saying, "Mosquitoes don't
bother me." And she, not understanding, had replied,
"You're lucky."

Now she laughed and touched her lips, just lightly, with
her tongue, savoring the lingering taste. Wasn't life filled
with the most incredible surprises?

She began pedaling back toward camp.